TRAPPED IN THE DARK DECADE

CREAKING CHAIR BOOKS

KAY RACE

TRAPPED IN THE DARK DECADE

Published by

Creaking Chair Books

First Edition 2018

Book One in The Dark Edinburgh Series

CONTENTS

1

" A JOURNEY INTO DARKNESS"

Kitty and Peter moved into a flat together in the summer of 1994, just after Kitty turned 40. She hadn't long returned from studying massage in New Zealand and was full of enthusiasm and was very optimistic about setting up a massage business. Until she was in a position to do so, she got a job as a clerk in the St Andrew Press, a publishing house which was a subsidiary of the Church of Scotland. She felt fortunate that she had secured a job so quickly after returning home. This 'good luck' reinforced her belief that the Universe was still smiling upon her.

Although she could not have known it then, they would never again have a flat so well situated or as well furnished as the one in Stockbridge, their first home together. It was in a newly built block and was ready to just move themselves and their clothes into. It was beautifully furnished and carpeted, complete with white goods. Their top floor windows boasted a magnificent view of the Castle and rooftops of the Royal Mile, even at that distance. Its southern facade made the place feel light and airy, the irony of which would dawn on Kitty before the year was out.

The luxury of their new accommodation did not come cheap and Kitty and Peter had to pay the usual month's rent in advance plus a month as deposit. There was also the estate agent's arrangement fee which all added up to a hefty sum. Peter had no savings to call on so Kitty cashed in an endowment policy to cover it. She'd been keeping the policy for a rainy day. Well, she thought, it looks like the rain has come on early and really didn't mind the inequity of providing the money, believing Peter would redress the balance in the near future.

Peter was a part time taxi driver, working only at the weekends. His burning ambition was to be picked for the Scottish Badminton team for the next Commonwealth Games which were to be held in Kuala Lumpur in 1998. This work pattern left him free to train Monday to Friday and afforded him a long term opportunity to develop his game and all that being chosen for the team would entail. He knew the competition for a team place would be fierce, but he was convinced this plan would give him as good a chance as anyone.

To Kitty's deep dismay, two patterns emerged over the first two to three months of them living together. Firstly, Kitty began to wonder about Peter's commitment to his sport and the four year training plan. She would return home from work around 5.30 and either find him still in bed or only just out of it. As the weeks went by and this routine, or rather lack of one, continued, she asked him if anything was troubling him. She thought that if she encouraged him he would return to what she believed had been his regular training regime. She didn't point out the obvious but approached it in a way she thought was supportive. He would become moody and say there was nothing wrong and to stop going on about it. She was beginning to become aware of his indolent nature.

The other pattern that gradually manifest was what she came to know as his controlling behaviour. He frowned upon her friendships and social life. Kitty had been a popular member of staff at Lothian Regional Council and had kept in touch with friends there when she was away and had reconnected with them on her return to Edinburgh. She would either meet up with them in town on Friday evenings or have them to the flat for a meal. She was famous for her 'Baked potato and Australian wine nights'. Peter started putting in an appearance at Kitty's 'at homes' and act like the Spectre at the Feast. The inevitable result was that Kitty's invitations began to be turned down until she stopped issuing them altogether. She still met her friends in town but the cost of this began to outweigh the enjoyment. At first she had thought, why shouldn't she meet her friends on a Friday? Why should she live like a nun because he chose to work a Friday night shift? He started coming home just when she was about to leave for town and he would look her up and down and shake his head, as though sad and disappointed with a favourite child. He would tell her that her clothes and makeup made her look like a street walker. Incredulous, she would look critically at her image in the mirror, since immediately before his arrival she thought she looked okay. On those nights she would arrive late with a tear-stained face and her friends would try to reassure her that she looked wonderful ... and respectable. In the end, the fallout from persisting in meeting her friends, forced her to think that the few hours of pleasure weren't worth the days of bad moods afterwards. Kitty grew tired of the constant battle and, if she were to be honest, she knew her friends were finding her unreliable. Not only did she not invite friends home, she stopped going out with them altogether. This was the beginning of Peter's plan for keeping Kitty socially isolated. She did keep in touch with Charles who had been a friend for years and she wasn't giving him up without a fight, although she knew Peter hated him because he was gay.

In the short space of three months or so, he had ground down her spirit and her enthusiasm for life. She began to yearn for the life she'd had in New Zealand, when she had the freedom to be herself, truly herself and not the woman Peter seemed intent on moulding her into. Her plans for her massage business were left in cold storage for the duration.

Peter's lack of exercise and fitness seemed to make him irritable and he was often sharp with Kitty and made unkind comments. She began to lose her self confidence with his constant put-downs and criticisms. He had started going to the sports centre when Kitty came home from work, not to train, but to meet up with friends who worked during the day and trained in the evenings. He would come home and talk about female athletes and sportswomen he saw there, making lewd remarks or telling her how he "wouldn't mind fucking her". Kitty tried to tell him that this wasn't just hurtful to her, but disrespectful to the women he was objectifying. This had made him angry, not only because he probably didn't know what the phrase meant, but because he disliked being judged and found wanting. She was totally unprepared for his reaction to the disapproval she'd voiced. He man-handled her to the floor, straddled her and shouted angry obscenities into her face. She was frightened and confused as she had never seen this side of him. He got up off her and threw something at her before leaving the room. It hit her with an almighty wallop on the wrist which became a very tender, bruised lump.

She sat stunned, feeling as though she had been plunged into an alien world. She asked herself, how had this happened? This was the beginning of the physical abuse, the use of force to bend her to his will.

Towards the end of November Peter was struggling to pay his share of the rent and utilities. Rather than having the expense of a telephone, they used the box on the corner of the street, such was the pressure on their finances. Of course, Kitty thought, if he worked proper hours it wouldn't be so difficult. He neither worked nor trained during the days of Monday to Friday.

Peter decided they should move to a cheaper flat and so they scoured the 'To Let' advertisements in the Edinburgh Evening News for the next week. They found a flat in a cheaper area, which was rather a come down from both the flat and the area they'd been living in. However, Kitty knew better than to complain about their change of circumstances.

JUST BEFORE CHRISTMAS PETER had taken on extra shifts a few evenings a week to earn a bit more money. Naively, Kitty wondered whether it was to get a Christmas present for her. Kitty loved the festive season and bought and sent cards to family and what was left of her friends. One evening a few days before Christmas, Kitty had made and decorated a little Christmas cake complete with marzipan and icing for Peter's parents, as they were visiting them the following evening. She had just finished decorating it and was sitting on the sofa when Peter came home. She had asked him how his shift had gone when he rushed at her and grabbed her by the throat. It was so sudden that she didn't have time to struggle and she quickly lost consciousness. He must have let go of his hold on her and when she came to she was puzzled and perplexed by Peter's lack of concern. He didn't apologise and when she asked him why he had done it he grunted,

"I had a crap night and you were sitting looking so fucking pleased with yourself, it pissed me off." Hurt she replied,

"I was pleased because I had finished the Christmas cake for *your* parents. Please don't take your rotten shifts out on me Peter." His response was to grab her face and squeeze hard, snarling,

"Well stop looking so fucking smug in future." He shoved her back against the sofa and went to bed. Shocked, Kitty sat rubbing her face, knowing it would probably be bruised by morning.

The following day Kitty was still in a state of shock and wondered whether she had dreamt the whole episode. Peter who was, surprisingly, in a better frame of mind, apologised and promised it would never happen again.

That Christmas was the worst Kitty had ever experienced. It was more of a non-event really, since Peter didn't like the festive season. He worked on Christmas Day leaving her at home without the comfort of Christmas dinner, it was just like any other day. She didn't get so much as a card from him. She didn't know it at the time, but that's what the following nine Christmas Days would be like.

2

"TILL DEATH DO US PART"

For Kitty, 1994 ended very differently than she had anticipated at the beginning of the year and when she had returned from New Zealand in the summer. The light and airy-ness of the new flat had failed to penetrate the dark deeds happening within its walls and the new one reflected her dismal life.

Peter was not the man he had convinced her he was, in fact, he was the person she had felt such antipathy towards the previous year. How had her instincts betrayed her so?

However, in January 1995 the more pleasant Peter had rallied, perhaps the result of a new year resolution? Whatever it was, he was behaving better and he vowed to Kitty that he wanted to start afresh in everything; their relationship and his training plan. He also asked her to marry him as a way of proving his commitment to her. She was initially astonished and unsure, but his earnestness was so convincing, she agreed, naively hopeful that it would prove a turning point after their 'false start'.

They were to be married in a Registry Office in Edinburgh. He persuaded Kitty that it would be more romantic to do it that way and to keep it a secret. There was to be no fuss, no wedding outfits, no flowers and no guests. The real reason for the secrecy, she later realised, was that he didn't want his mother to know, whom he knew disapproved of Kitty, as no woman would be good enough for her 'little boy'.

On a wet Wednesday in February 1995 they were married by the Queen Street Registrar. Their only witnesses were two members of staff who worked in the building. Kitty would look back on her wedding to Peter and think two things: that it was a very poor excuse for a wedding day, which is meant to be the most special day of a woman's life; and that the weather that day was an omen of the dark and dreich years which would follow.

It was around this time Peter told Kitty he thought it would be a good idea for her to give up her full time job and get a weekend night shift to coincide with his shifts. Compliant, as it was always easier that way since Peter always got what he wanted in the end, she found a job in a takeaway franchise in the Waverley station where she worked from 10pm to 6am on Friday and Saturday nights. This meant she was free to 'coach' him from Monday to Friday. Peter believed his training plan was now back on track.

Their routine was to be up early each morning and go to the sports centre where they would follow the programme that Peter had prepared. He maintained, in his annoyingly pedantic way, that each day was the foundation for the following one and, as such, they had to stick meticulously to the programme. Kitty, who felt totally out of her depth, tried to be what he wanted her to be: his personal coach. She read the books and watched the videos he had given her on badminton technique. To Kitty's utter surprise, despite having no savings to contribute towards the cost of their first flat, he produced £200 to buy a video camera. Kitty was to video his training sessions and then he would analyse the recording to see what needed to be improved upon.

Sometimes the work went to plan, but there were days or even weeks when, according to Peter, something went wrong and so the whole week was forfeited. Kitty found this very difficult and felt, on those occasions, that she was summoning up the energy and enthusiasm for both of them. The reason for such 'blips' could be something as simple as being 15 minutes 'late' for their scheduled departure for the sports centre. She was beginning to feel really frustrated by these interruptions to *his programme*, but said nothing. It seemed to ring of a saying she had heard once ... for the want of a nail ... Anyway, to her mind it was sheer madness.

Since the training plan was foundering, Kitty decided to leave the Friday and Saturday night shift work. She found a job as a care assistant in a residential home run by The Little Sisters of the Poor in Gilmore Place. She worked Saturday and Sunday afternoons there and she was very happy in the serene environment. For six hours each Saturday and Sunday she was free from Peter's oppressive and obsessive moods and, as such, to Kitty, it didn't feel like work at all. It also left her free Mondays to Fridays, although Peter hadn't trained in a while. She felt valued working for the nuns and they paid her extra to come in and do abdominal massage to help reduce the residents' dependence on laxatives.

Peter's newest plan for Kitty's career was announced in spring. He said that she should study 'The Knowledge' and become a taxi driver working weekend day shifts, as he was now doing. Kitty wasn't sure she wanted to do this but life was much more pleasant if she complied, so she started the long task of learning, not only the streets of Edinburgh, but theatres, hospitals, cinemas, cemeteries, overseas Consulates etc. In addition to all of this, she had to know the quickest routes from A to B. Kitty was a quick study and found it a bit like the quizzes she had loved as a child, however this was a project that would take a few months to complete, before finally sitting the test.

By early summer that year, Kitty and Peter's financial situation was in a serious state and, to help out, Kitty took on a second job cleaning in the City Chambers. In addition to working Saturday and Sunday for the nuns, she worked from 6-9am Monday to Friday, which meant getting up a 5 o'clock during the week.

ONE MORNING IN AUGUST, less than six months after their marriage, Kitty returned home just after 9am to have a little sleep with Peter who was never up when she finished work. She awoke feeling amorous but Peter repelled her attentions. Hurt, she accepted that he wasn't 'in the mood'. He suggested going to the John Muir country park on the East Lothian coast and Kitty agreed as it was one of her favourite places to visit.

On the journey there, Kitty had a distinct feeling of unease, a tangible undercurrent which was emanating from Peter. They parked the car and followed the path through the woods towards the beach. About twenty minutes into the walk Peter dropped the bombshell. He stopped walking and told Kitty that he had had sex with a prostitute in the taxi the previous night. Kitty stood rigid, frozen in shock. Her mind went back to last night when he had come home from work. She had been studying The Knowledge and had fallen asleep. She woke to the sound of him in the bathroom which was unusual since he normally came into the living room first. When she asked him, half asleep, what he was doing, he said he had spilled diesel on his hands and was washing it off. She realised now that it wasn't diesel he was trying to wash off his hands, it was guilt!

Her shock gave way to anger at this disclosure of his betrayal and she started beating him on the chest. He quickly quelled the 'attack', if it could be called that. Using a stick he had picked up earlier, Peter quickly stood behind her and pressed it to her throat. He said, menacingly, into her ear,

"I could kill you here and now and nobody would know." Kitty rightly felt that she was in great danger on this deserted beach. He threw the stick away, having achieved his intention: to put the fear of death into her. Feeling dizzy from the shock and the stick across her throat, she fell silent. The anger was replaced by a deep gnawing pain in her gut.

They walked back to the car in silence as her imagination worked overtime on the events of the night before. As he drove them back to Edinburgh, Kitty knew that her life and relationship with Peter had changed forever. The trust he had broken could never be fully repaired, even if she did forgive him in time. Despite the beautiful, sunny summer day, Kitty felt a dark cloud looming over her and the brightness of the day seemed to mock her. Just as they entered the city's eastern limits, Kitty told Peter calmly that she needed to know all the details of last night, otherwise her imagination would drive her mad. She was quite taken aback when he agreed and related the evening's 'activities'. He told Kitty that he had gone to a place, near the docks at the Port of Leith, where it was well known that sex could be purchased. He had pulled up at the kerb, close to where a woman was standing, rolled down the window and asked her if she was looking for work. She approached the taxi and asked him what he was interested in and reeled off prices for 'full sex, hand and blow jobs'. He 'treated' himself to the deluxe version offered.

That evening after Peter had gone to work, Kitty could not settle. She couldn't stay in the flat alone with such devastating knowledge so raw in her mind. She changed into what had once been her 'night out' clothes and went out on the town. She had a meal and a few glasses of wine in an Italian restaurant in Hanover Street. This was a bitter-sweet experience, since it had been a favourite eating place for Kitty and her friends before Peter came along.

Later that night, when Peter returned from work around midnight, he asked her where she had been since she wasn't at home when he popped in around 9 o'clock. Wearily, she told him where she had gone and, surprisingly, he left it at that.

The following evening when Peter came home, he was not at all pleased to find Kitty with her eyes red and swollen from crying. His displeasure soon turned to anger as he said,

"What the fuck have you been crying for." Perplexed, Kitty replied,

"Peter can't you understand how painful this is for me? It's the last thing I expected of you after your disapproval of your friend, David Yates, having an affair." A sob caught in her throat as the pain of the betrayal hit her afresh. Growing more angry, he shouted in her face,

"It's not the same fucking thing, is it? Live with it and stop your whining." By this time she was crying huge hiccuping sobs as she crouched into the corner of the sofa. Her continued crying enraged him and he began to plunge a large kitchen knife into the cushion by her head. Terrified she covered her face with her hands and then he suddenly changed tack and silenced her by putting his hands around her throat, pushing her backwards into the sofa. She thought she was going to lose consciousness as he snarled, "Die bitch!"

She didn't know where the strength came from, but she succeeded in prising the fingers of one of his hands away from her throat. Maddened by this act of defiance, he grabbed her hand and bit down viciously on one of her fingers. She screamed as she felt an agonising pain. His reply was a sharp whack across her cheek, then he went off to bed, the matter settled as far as he was concerned.

THE FOLLOWING MORNING Kitty got up after Peter had gone out. Her finger was swollen and bruised and very painful. When she tried to bend it, the pain of the movement gave her a sick feeling in the pit of her stomach, which worried her.

Being Saturday, she had arranged to meet her sister Anna in Princes Street to look around the shops and get some lunch before going to work in the home at 1.30. By the second shop, Kitty was in so much pain that she told Anna she would have to go to the A&E at the Royal Infirmary. She had told Anna that the bathroom door had banged shut on her finger when a gust of wind from the open window had caught it.

She was x-rayed at the hospital and was told she had a spiral fracture of the ring finger. When asked by staff what had happened, she told them the truth. She was a bit taken aback when no comment was made or suggestion that she should go to the police. But then, she thought, they must see this kind of thing all the time. They put a splint on it and said it would take 6-8 weeks to heal. Kitty was off work for 7 weeks as both her jobs required her hands to be fit for the work.

Her lost earnings from both jobs cost Kitty in excess of £400; the real cost of a '£30 fuck' with a prostitute, she thought crudely. The price of cheating is dear indeed, and that was merely the financial cost.

Peter never did apologise for breaking her finger.

3

"HELL'S ROLLERCOASTER"

1996-1999

K itty had been driving the taxi for some months. She had sat and passed the Knowledge test in October of the previous year and her taxi license had come through in November. It was with some sadness that she gave notice to the nuns that she would be leaving their employment at the end of November. Her first day behind the wheel of a black hackney cab was set for early December. Through Peter's enquiries she had secured a Saturday and Sunday driving job on a 50:50 basis. This meant that she and the owner (who drove the taxi during the week) would split her 'takings'. The cost of fuelling up the taxi came from the owner's share.

Her first day was coming ever closer and Kitty was beginning to feel very nervous.

"Why did I let him talk me into this?" She asked herself out loud, although she knew that she had just gone along with another of Peter's schemes for making money. It was one thing 'driving' a taxi in theory, she thought, and another actually doing it. She had passed the Knowledge test with 100%, she reminded herself as a confidence booster, a fact which hadn't gone down too well with Peter who had attained just above the 90% pass mark. She had planned what she would wear on her first day as she knew being 'well dressed' helped her to feel more confident. Her sister Anna had bought her a sorely needed new pair of shoes which were elegant and comfortable.

The day inevitably arrived and Peter dropped Kitty off at her pick up point in Portobello at exactly 6am. Most taxi day shifts were 6am to 6pm which, at that time of year, meant beginning and ending the working day in the dark. Driving a manual transmission taxi for this length of time was wearing on the body, especially the knees, with all the stopping and starting at traffic lights, which in Edinburgh, seemed to be at regular 400 yard intervals.

As a way to ease into her new job, Peter had suggested that Kitty should go on the rank at the bottom of Dundas Street which was relatively quiet on a Saturday morning. She found it quite nerve-wracking that first day whenever a passenger hopped in and asked to be taken somewhere. She had to think fast to recall exactly where the destination was and work out the quickest route to it. The public didn't like to think they're being taken for a longer ride than necessary while the meter was ticking. To complicate matters, particularly at first, the taxi was radio controlled and sometimes jobs would be given over the radio. Initially, she felt a bit daft saying "copy", to indicate that she had noted the details, and "over" when the exchange had ended.

Her favourite jobs were 'contracts'. This happened when an account holder would pay the taxi company directly for journeys. Since the passengers did not pay, there was no quibbling over the cheapest or fastest route. The best, by far, were the hospital ones, where people or specimens were taken from site to site.

At that time, Kitty was one of only a handful of female taxi drivers in the city and, although most people were favourable, some would try to ridicule, usually male passengers. Many women liked to see the elegant driver, that Kitty always presented as, commenting that many of the male drivers were short, fat, smelly men who leered at them from the rear view mirror.

One of main negative aspects of this work however, was that she often saw Peter during the course of the day, either in passing or on one of the many taxi ranks in Edinburgh. On one occasion, whilst standing talking to him through the cab window during a quiet period, she noticed a pornographic magazine lying beside his work bag. She asked, in a shocked, harsh tone, as she pointed to the offending article,

"What's that doing in your taxi?" Looking sheepish he stammered,

"Oh that! It was left on the back seat and I haven't had time to put it in a bin." Kitty didn't believe him, but she didn't challenge him further. However, he knew by the set expression on her face, that she wasn't happy or convinced. Later events would prove that her suspicions were well founded.

THE TIME SPENT in Peter's company over the years made Kitty acutely aware of the way he looked at women, especially young, blonde women. He didn't just glance surreptitiously but openly stared at their chests. Kitty dreaded summer when many women wore scantier and more revealing clothes. In exasperation one sunny day, while they were standing by their taxis, Kitty brought it to his attention immediately after he'd ogled the breasts of a young woman who had just walked by. He swore blind that he hadn't. Kitty found this behaviour very cruel and very dismissive of her feelings. Often, when they were in the car, it would be women that they were passing in the street he would stare at and Kitty cringed every time. It got so difficult for her that she would look in the opposite direction so she didn't have to see. However, she always knew when he was doing it as he went through a little repertoire, either of forced enthusiasm for something totally unrelated, or else he became over-cheerful, which certainly wasn't something he could normally be described as. Kitty thought it was a pretty pathetic attempt to distract her from what he was doing.

In the flat one afternoon, Kitty tried talking to Peter about it because she found it very hurtful and it was eating away at her, already poor, self esteem and her sense of herself as a woman. He was immediately on the defensive so, playing safe, Kitty tried to change the subject and went to prepare vegetables for their tea. He must have been simmering for some time so that Kitty jumped when he quietly came up behind her as she stood at the sink peeling potatoes. She had the small vegetable knife in her hand which he grabbed, closing his hand tightly over hers, and forced it to her throat. She could feel the sharp blade against her skin as he said quietly,

"So you don't like me looking at other women eh? If you weren't such an ugly old hag I wouldn't have to. You're pissing me off so much now, that I could happily slit your scrawny throat." Kitty tried desperately to resist the force of his hand, but he was too strong. Suddenly, he released his grip on her, pleased at how frightened she had been. Kitty, her heart racing, fought back the hot tears knowing he would use them as an excuse to torment her further. After that encounter, Kitty tried to close her mind to his lascivious leering.

· · ·

IN THE SPRING OF 1997, Peter moved them, yet again, to another flat. It was cheaper than the previous one and it certainly showed in the furniture, if it could be described as such. The saying "you get what you pay for" was certainly true in this case, mice and all. Kitty was losing track of all the addresses they'd had in the three short years they had been together. Smiling ruefully, she thought that, rather than short, those years felt like heavy decades to her. By then she was pretty ground down, physically and emotionally, by Peter's controlling and offensive behaviour. She slept badly and jumped at the least sudden noise. She was constantly and continually apologising. She apologised when she did something 'wrong' in his opinion, or if she didn't do something he thought she should have. Damned if she did and damned if she didn't. She felt like a gibbering wreck a lot of the time.

Peter's moods became increasingly unpredictable and Kitty became highly sensitised to any nuances. She became hyper-vigilant and was always prepared for 'flight'. Forget the 'fight' response to the threat of danger, he was too powerful and Kitty had learned, by experience, the futility of it. She would often walk around the dark streets of their neighbourhood because she felt safer there than at home, when his 'just below the surface' anger was palpable and she couldn't know how it might manifest.

Alert now to Kitty's quick exits, Peter was always ready to stop her leaving the flat. He often caught her as she tried to get through the half open door. He would force the door hard against her arm or leg or whatever was part way through. She realised he was playing mind games with her, like a cat playing cruelly with a mouse.

Threats came in various forms: non-verbal, as in a tangible undercurrent when she could almost smell and taste it in the room; sometimes it would be a cryptic statement, all the more frightening as she was never sure how to interpret its meaning. Either way, Kitty knew it spelled danger. She came home one afternoon and, although he was still in bed, she immediately sensed a threat. She about-turned, ran out of the flat and downstairs into the street. Fortunately, she had the car keys still in her hand, so acutely perceptive was she to any danger she hadn't put them on the hook behind the door. She knew he couldn't follow her straight away since he was naked. The car was a couple of streets away, parking being difficult in the city centre, and she ran to where it was parked, looking behind in terror of Peter pursuing her. She stopped a woman in the street and told her she was worried she was being followed and asked her to accompany her to the car. The woman asked Kitty if she knew the person and nodded understanding when she said it was her husband. It transpired, when Kitty finally got home, that Peter hadn't bothered to dress and follow her.

PETER REGULARLY CAME up with ideas for making 'easy' money and Kitty went along with them for the sake of peace and safety. One such venture was delivering the free 'Edinburgh Advertiser' to tenements in the area they lived in. Kitty found it exhausting as, not only were the papers heavy to carry, but some of the tenements were four storeys high. The extent to which Kitty had lost a grip on reality is illustrated by the fact that she didn't think it odd to be doing this on the afternoon following their marriage in the morning.

Peter's daftest scheme of all had to be the abortive stair-cleaning idea, with the slogan, "We Don't Cut Corners, We

Clean Them!" He got Kitty to type and print flyers advertising their 'service' and they trudged around tenement buildings posting them through letterboxes. A few days later, they followed up by knocking on doors to enquire if anyone was interested. Nobody was. Not to be beaten, Peter came up with the idea of giving a free demonstration of their work. He chose the stair that Kitty's sister, Denise, lived in at Tollcross, they would need to get hot water from somebody so it made sense. Kitty swept the stair from top to bottom, all 4 flights, landings and front and back passages, while Peter mopped. Again, nobody, except Denise, was interested. Thus ended their stair cleaning enterprise.

IN SEPTEMBER THAT YEAR, forever on the lookout for cheaper and cheaper accommodation, Peter had the 'bright' idea that they should buy a static caravan and they would have only the ground rent to pay. He had found one advertised in the Edinburgh Evening News for £1900 cash payment. Kitty protested saying,

"But Peter, we don't even have 1900 pennies."

"*But Peter, we don't even have 1900 pennies.*" He mocked in a high pitched tone, then in his normal voice, he replied dismissively,

"You can ask your sister Anna for a loan and we can pay her back so much a month until it's paid off." To him it was simple. Kitty was dubious, for a start she hated the idea of asking her sister for a loan, it was so embarrassing. He cajoled and bullied her until finally she gave in. She took her courage in both hands and phoned Anna from a phone box and asked for a loan of £1900. At first, Anna wasn't keen, but said she would think about it. A few days later Anna agreed and sent Kitty a cheque.

They went to see the advertised caravan which was situated in a static home park a few miles south of Edinburgh and Kitty was utterly dismayed by its state of disrepair. The walls which had once divided the kitchen and living room had been removed, making it 'open plan'. There were no floor coverings throughout, just the exposed plywood sections of floor. The shower room, which had the toilet in, was tiny and the bedroom was quite dark, despite there being no curtains on the window. It was a 'dump', Kitty thought and had difficulty imagining herself actually living in this mean space. Peter was as enthusiastic as Kitty was unimpressed and he seemed taken in by the woman owner who had the 'gift of the gab'. The deal was done, without any haggling or even looking at other static homes to compare value for money, since, by this point, Kitty was too exhausted by life with Peter to complain or even care.

They moved into the 'shell' of a home, bringing only a few bits and pieces with them and just a mattress on the floor to sleep on. Over the following two years, there were very few 'home improvements', even the curtains Anna gave them were actually nailed above the window frames and hooked back during the day, as Peter couldn't be bothered putting up curtain rails even if they'd had spare money to buy them. It's no surprise that they discouraged people from visiting them.

Whilst living in the caravan park, Peter gave up his weekend taxi shifts in favour of a Monday to Friday day shift 'rental'. This meant giving the taxi owner a fixed sum each week and Peter would keep all the takings and pay for the diesel he used himself. He told Kitty enthusiastically,

"If I work 12 hours a day, I'll be able to make a few hundred pounds a week, easily." He already had the money 'in the bank', Kitty thought incredulously. The reality, unfortunately, was somewhat different. Some days he would go out and come home early if business was slow and, when Kitty looked shocked, he would say that he had the rest of the week to make up the money. Before long he was going out for only a few hours some days and not at all on others. Soon the cost of the rental was more than Peter was earning. Kitty, who was still working part time, was extremely worried, the phone had already been disconnected. The loan payments to Anna faltered and they were living from hand to mouth.

IN THE AUTUMN of 1999 two things happened: Peter went back to his previous weekend day shift on a 50:50 basis, which was obviously more sustainable for his limited application to work; and he had a bad falling out with the caravan site manager. He decided they would 'move on' again. This was the start of moving further and further away from Edinburgh and family. They moved to an unfurnished flat in Peebles, which was owned by the Church of Scotland. It was a nice enough flat and had the twin advantages of being a cheaper rent and carpeted throughout, which to Kitty, was sheer luxury after the caravan.

The disadvantage, for Kitty however, was that it foreshadowed her removal to becoming georgraphically isolated, as they would move again and again, until they were in the very remote lodge house deep in the Scottish Borders.

4

AUTUMN 1999

"A PRISON WITHOUT BARS"

Not long after Peter announced his decision to move to the Borders, Kitty sat in Tesco's café eating her vegetarian breakfast of poached eggs, mushrooms, tomatoes and hash browns, drinking her second pot of tea. She was making the breakfast last as long as possible to delay returning home to Peter and whatever mood she might find him in.

Kitty was now 45, but looked and felt older, her permed hair - the perm being a gift from her sister Helena - was almost totally white. She was five foot, three and very slightly built, she looked like a strong puff of wind could blow her over. She was tidily dressed and, although her clothes were clean and pressed, they were obviously hand-me-downs. Her polished shoes were 'down at heel' which was a fair reflection of her life in general.

She had wrested this time from Peter by telling him she had an appointment first thing with the gynaecology consultant at the Royal Infirmary. The look of utter distaste which spread across his face meant that she didn't have to provide any detail or proof and, in this way, she had managed to win some time out and away from his moody clutches. She had left him still sleeping when she quietly let herself out of the caravan at 8.30am and was in town in time for the shops opening. After an enjoyable trip around Morningside's many Charity Shops, which was all Kitty could afford to look at - even window shopping, she felt ready for something to eat. She relished the meal she had just eaten since having an appetite in Peter's presence was rare to non-existent. For the past four years or so, he had complained about the way she ate and drank, telling her that it disgusted him. Consequently, she ate very little in front of him, hence her wraith-like stature.

Pushing that thought to the back of her mind, she looked out of the window overlooking the car park and watched the busy shoppers. It was still fairly early on this Monday morning and the customers were mainly women. Kitty imagined their perfect lives with loving husbands and happy, clever children.

Suddenly it occurred to her that, to another person's eyes, she might look like the women she was watching with, just a touch of, envy. However, as she knew well, appearances could be deceptive and you couldn't know what went on behind closed doors. No, she thought shaking her head, on closer inspection, nobody would take her for a happy wife and mother, not with the dark circles under her faded blue eyes, the strained look on her face or the hunched posture, indicative of self protection. She rather thought anyone observing her would think that she had a haunted look about her. They would be right.

To Kitty, it felt like a hundred years ago that she had felt vibrant, confident and had nothing more to worry her than what she would wear next day. She asked herself, what had happened to the woman she once was, the woman who was in love with life, who met challenges head-on rather than constantly fearing problems and difficult situations? Sighing, she looked back over the years, trying to see through the grey mists of time. Strangely, she couldn't see herself in her mind's eye, her vision could not penetrate the dense fog of pain, humiliation and the panic of abject fear. Instead, she somehow 'felt' the memory of her former self and the definite sense of its gradual dissolution, like a morning mist evaporating with the sun. What had happened to her? Of course, the simple answer was that *He* had happened, although it was rather more complex than that. However, the indisputable fact was that he was central to the process of her fall into this desperate state.

She felt overwhelmingly trapped and wondered how much longer she could stand this life of constantly walking on eggshells and trying to avoid the fear, humiliation and threat of violence which had, for a long time, been her day to day existence. She felt great shame at this 'ghost' of a person she had become. She stumbled and teetered, emotionally and mentally, under the weight of this secret, which she kept hidden from the world. She also felt desperately lonely and longed for someone to rescue her since she no longer had the physical or mental energy to change how things were. There were so many nights now that she went to bed hoping that she would not waken up in the morning.

5

"FADING LIGHT"

2000-2002

They hadn't been in Peebles for more than a few months when Kitty started experiencing feelings of increasing anxiety and dread. She continued to sleep badly and would be awake during the early hours of the morning, feeling something akin to despair, a despair that she would never feel 'normal' or well again, and that this existence would continue to be hell on earth for the foreseeable future. She was tired all the time and was unable to do more than drag herself from day to dreary day. She felt as though she was sleep walking through a mire of misery and fatigue, in which she constantly stumbled trying to avoid the psychological traps that Peter seemed to have set at every turn. She had even begun to wonder whether she might be going mad. Several times lately, she hadn't been able to find something where she was sure she had previously laid it down and then, after a thorough search of the flat, she would find it in the most obscure place. She always left her watch on the dresser before getting into bed and then, last Wednesday morning, when she went to put it on after her shower, it wasn't there. Puzzled, she checked the window sill in case she had left it there, but she hadn't. She asked Peter,

"Have you seen my watch? I put it on the dresser before going to bed last night, but it's not there now." He replied,

"No I haven't seen it, you must have left it somewhere else. You're getting a bit absent-minded these days." He turned away then so she didn't see the wicked, smug smile on his face. She shrugged and said,

"I'll just have to start searching since I don't feel dressed without it." Kitty searched in the obvious places first, she looked under and behind the dresser, in case it had somehow been knocked off. There was no joy there, so she systematically emptied the drawers in case she had put it somewhere 'daft'.

Two hours later, looking in the less obvious places, she came across it on top of the electricity meter in the hall cupboard. She called to Peter that she had found it and when he asked her where, she said,

"Would you believe, it was in the electricity cupboard? How on earth did it get there? I haven't been in there since I put the power card in." She had an uneasy feeling as he casually replied,

"I told you it would be in a stupid place, you need to pay attention to where you leave your belongings or you'll be getting 'put away'." In the other room, he was smiling at the amount of time it had taken Kitty to find her watch and, especially, for making her doubt her sanity. She had the strong suspicion that Peter had been the engineer of the items she had supposedly 'misplaced' recently, although she couldn't prove it. She would keep a wary eye on him from now on.

Ironically, the only time she felt she had any energy was when the adrenaline coursed through her body in response to Peter's threats and abuse, like just the other day when he'd pushed her against the wall, spitting and swearing in her face for whatever 'indiscretion' she may have committed. His rough handling left bruises, usually from his tight grip of whatever part of her body he had grabbed. This meant covering up with clothes, even in the heat of summer. Although she wanted more energy, she certainly didn't want it from this source.

She had continued with the weekend shifts, which meant getting up at 4.30am to travel to Edinburgh with Peter for a 12 hour day driving the taxi and putting on a cheerful face for her passengers.

By the spring of 2000, Kitty had literally ground to a standstill. She registered with the local medical practice and made an appointment to see a doctor later in the week. She was hoping they could give her a tonic or something to liven her up.

At the consultation she saw a woman doctor who listened carefully and sympathetically as Kitty described how she was feeling. Despite the doctor's gentle probing, Kitty could not bring herself to disclose her awful life with Peter. Peter had insisted on taking her to the appointment and wasn't at all pleased when she went in to see the doctor alone. On the way there he had said that he would come in with her as he was 'concerned' about her health, Kitty said nothing, which he took for compliance, he knew his presence would prevent her from spilling the 'domestic' beans. However, when the doctor called her name, she turned to Peter and said,

"You wait here, I shouldn't be too long." and followed the doctor into the consulting room. She could see by the murderous look on his face that he was furious, but being in a public place he just grunted agreement. She had that sinking feeling of knowing she would probably pay for this piece of defiance later.

After assessing Kitty, the doctor said that, in addition to exhaustion, she was depressed. She advised Kitty to give up the taxi job and wrote her a 'sick note' for two months, during which time she was to rest and avoid stress. In her mind, Kitty said, 'as if, living with Peter!' She also prescribed a daily dose of 20 mg of the antidepressant, Fluoxetine. Kitty realised that the tablets weren't going to change the sad state that was her life, but maybe they would help her feel more able to cope with Peter's bad moods and behaviour.

On the way home from the surgery Peter was moodily quiet, obviously brooding over what he regarded as Kitty 'putting one over on him'. However, once in the flat, he seemed to have forgotten her 'misdemeanour' and he talked about things as though nothing had happened. Kitty felt a huge wave of relief wash over her and thought that was the end of the matter.

It was in the evening that Peter meted out his 'punishment'. After tea, he suggested going for a drive as it was a lovely evening and the daylight would last a while longer. Unsuspecting, Kitty happily agreed.

Their flat was in School Brae and they drove west along the High Street and on to the A72, heading into the countryside of the Tweed Valley. Kitty had always enjoyed seeing new places and was interested in the passing scenery. Several miles on, Peter turned onto a single track road and stopped the car unexpectedly a few minutes later. Kitty looked at Peter, puzzled as to why they had stopped. The look on his face, which she had recently begun to regard as ugly, warned her that trouble was brewing. She felt her stomach turn to water as he said,

"You thought you'd got away with it, didn't you?" Kitty answered,

"I don't know what you mean, got away with what?" He turned to her and squeezed her shoulder hard, causing her to wince with pain and said,

"You agreed with me coming in with you to see that doctor, what did you tell her that you didn't want me to hear? You double crossed me, you bitch!" Trying to sound reasonable and appeasing Kitty replied,

"Actually Peter, if you remember, I didn't say anything either way and I didn't tell her anything other than my symptoms." He hit her cheek so hard with the back his hand, that her head snapped sharply away from him. In a menacing tone he said,

"Are you frightened? ... You should be. I could kill you and dump you here in the middle of nowhere. It could be years before your body was found ... if at all." She said quickly,

"I'm sorry, it won't happen again, I promise. You can come in with me next time." Leaning over, he released her seatbelt and, opening the door, shoved her bodily out of the car. He turned the car around and sped off, tyres squealing, in the direction they'd come from.

She could hardly believe he had abandoned her in this remote spot with no money to get a bus, should one even come along at this time of night. The sun was sinking and the shadows of the trees were long. Kitty shrugged in resignation at this incident, (but also at her life in general) and made her way back along the track towards the main road. When she reached it, the dusk was deepening and car lights were on full. Taking a deep breath and screwing up her courage, she began the walk homeward, hoping she wouldn't get hit by a car. There were no safety reflective strips on the jacket she was wearing.

Kitty had been walking along the A72 for about ten minutes when an approaching car signalled to pull in. Half hoping it was Peter coming back for her and half fearing a stranger with ill intent, she stepped onto the verge and waited. To her immense relief ... 'better the devil you know' ... it was Peter, who obviously thought she had learned her 'lesson' by now. She got in and thanked him. He nodded smugly and turned the car towards home.

IN JUNE THAT YEAR, they moved home again. The number of moves was making Kitty almost dizzy. This time they rented a cottage in the Yarrow Valley, in Selkirkshire, on the Bowhill estate. It was three miles from the historic town of Selkirk, which boasted one of the four Borders' Sheriff Courts. A statue of Sir Walter Scott stood outside the old Courthouse in the Square, which he had, in times past, presided over and where he had dispensed justice.

The new cottage which was accessed via a flight of stairs, was situated above the Gamekeeper's storeroom. It was rather sparsely furnished with the few possessions they had managed to accumulate since leaving furnished flats behind in Edinburgh for their many subsequent unfurnished properties.

Peter was still driving the taxi when they moved to Bowhill, but there were some weekends when he didn't go to work at all. This meant that the only money they had to live on was Kitty's sickness benefit. By early July, having missed work for a whole month, Peter told the taxi owner that he wasn't going back. He claimed he was depressed, although Kitty didn't see much evidence of it. He consulted a GP, in yet another new medical practice, and he was 'signed off' as 'unfit to work due to depression'.

The road tax was due and then became overdue as they didn't even have enough money to tax it for the shorter 6 month period. This left them stranded three miles from the nearest town with a bus service which ran once a day. Although she wasn't fully recovered herself, Kitty asked the doctor to sign her fit for work and she found a job as a carer working for Help At Home Borders, a home care organisation. Jean, the supervisor, was sympathetic to Kitty's circumstances and arranged her work accordingly. Kitty walked the three miles to work and back to see to the needs of her clients. Her duties were mainly housework for an elderly couple and she also helped the husband to shower and dress on alternate week days. Mrs Gibson always gave her a cup of tea and a piece of homemade cake after completing her work. Kitty found the duties for the other client more difficult as she didn't have the stomach for certain tasks, but persevered as she had to earn some money.

In September, when the benefits agency caught up with matters, they were informed that Kitty's earnings were to be deducted, almost pound for pound from Peter's benefit. Kitty gave up the care work as she was determined that she wasn't walking six miles to work and back for a wage which would, in effect, mean that she was working for about £5 a week. Thus Peter's benefit remained intact.

As the weeks went by, Peter became very friendly with Michael Littlejohn, the estate gamekeeper, and was offered 'cash in hand' to help with 'grouse beating'. Being the man of principle that he was, as Kitty sarcastically thought of him, he accepted the £20 a day to scare up innocent birds, for wealthy men to shoot at close range. Interestingly, Kitty noticed that his depression didn't affect him on those occasions.

Peter's behaviour towards Kitty hadn't changed but was modified for some of the time, while in the Littlejohns' company. Kitty enjoyed visiting Michael's wife and children and had spent many happy hours with them over the course of their stay at Bowhill, however she never spoke to Laura about the true nature of life with Peter. Laura herself, seemed to suffer somewhat from Michael's mercurial moods. There were times when they would all be in Laura's homely kitchen, drinking tea around the big farmhouse table and anyone would have thought that Kitty and Peter were a loving, happy couple. Peter played and joked with the four children and was the epitome of affability. However, a bird in the bush or a fly on their living room wall would hear a different story. Once out of the Littejohn's place his mood became sullen and irritable. It would happen so suddenly, he was contradictory and Kitty was becoming more aware of this quick change of mood and it bewildered her how he could go from happy to angry with what seemed like the flick of a switch. Similarly, when the Littlejohns visited them he was the perfect host, but once they'd said goodbye and shut the door, the pleasant facade was dropped and the ugly, moody face was back on. Kitty realised this also happened when her sisters paid their monthly visit, he was all sweetness and light, then when they had gone his dark cloud loomed over her again.

Winter of 2000-2001 was particularly cold in the valley and even the fast-flowing Ettrick nearby had frozen over. The Littljohns were good company and Kitty encouraged as much contact as possible since Peter's behaviour was better whilst in their presence. They went sledging one day, down a steep hill on the estate, which was the first fun and adventurous thing Kitty had done since her travels overseas. They returned to Laura's warm kitchen for hot chocolate and Kitty was almost happy during those brief hours of blissful respite from Peter's moods.

In March 2001, Kitty was astonished to learn that Peter's GP had referred him to the Community Mental Health Team since she hadn't noticed any significant change in his mental health despite increasing his medication. The team's Social Worker advised him to claim an additional benefit as he was by then assessed as having chronic depression. He was awarded the additional benefit which was backdated, so they received a cheque for a tidy sum. Kitty had mixed feelings about it since, on the one hand she didn't think he merited it, and, on the other, the money would buy a second hand car which would mean more freedom.

In April that year, very much to Kitty's dismay, Peter decided to move from Bowhill to another country cottage, this time on the Hirsel Estate near Coldstream. The distance from Selkirk made it difficult to keep in touch with their friends and Kitty was once again plunged into her grim life with Peter without any respite, other than the monthly visits from her sisters.

The Hirsel cottage wasn't as cosy as the one in Bowhill, having stone floors and only a coal fire in the living room for heating. Kitty looked back on the gas fire and central heating of their previous home as the ultimate in luxury, especially during the extremely cold winter of 2001-2002. They had no less than 3 'Calor Gas' heaters on the go that winter, as well as the coal fire, and they slept in the living room because it was too cold in the bedroom, with ice accumulating on the inside of the cottage windows.

It was around March time that Kitty was contacted by Jean, who had been her supervisor when she had worked for Help At Home Borders, offering her a job as a carer for a private client with dementia who needed help to shop and have meals prepared. Jean seemed to have a soft spot for Kitty and had kept in touch occasionally since Kitty had left her employment. Kitty wondered whether Jean had been through a similar experience to herself and had seen through Kitty's cheerful front. The private client was a wealthy lady with a minor title, who lived in a mansion-sized, albeit rundown, house set within acres of woodland and gardens. Jean's son-in-law, Tommy, was the other person involved in Mrs A's care and in addition to a good hourly rate of pay, Kitty would receive travel expenses, not just for taking Mrs A about, but to and from work. Kitty accepted the offer with alacrity and felt pleased that Jean had thought her worthy of this offer.

As Kitty had expected, her main duties were to take Mrs A out to shop in the village for her lunch or to the post office to collect her pension. The job provided Kitty with an opportunity to put some money aside for herself. She didn't tell Peter how much she actually earned and every week she 'salted' away the balance of what he believed her wages to be, in a dresser drawer. Kitty enjoyed watching the amount grow. She wasn't sure what she was saving for, but she had the vague notion that it might help change her circumstances at some future date.

In March 2002, they moved yet again, to a farm cottage owned by a large country estate, some miles east of Kelso.

6

"THE DARKNESS DEEPENS"

2002-2004

Working for Mrs A brightened Kitty's life considerably, mainly because she spent time away from Peter but also because Mrs A was a lovely, if eccentric, old lady.

When Kitty was on duty she would arrive at Forestdean House via the long drive through the woods which blocked out a lot of the light. On approaching the house she was suddenly plunged into the brightness of the day as she left the last of the trees behind.

On hearing the doorbell, Mrs A would look out of her first floor bedroom window to see who was there and, recognising Kitty, she would eagerly run downstairs like a woman decades younger and fling open the front door. She invariably had her A4 diary tucked under one arm and her first words to Kitty were always to ask her what the date was. She would then consult the diary to see what they were doing that day. Kitty and Tommy always entered the following day's activities in her diary.

Kitty's first task was to make sure Mrs A's cat was fed. She had, rather unimaginatively, named the cat "Pussy".

Once Pussy's needs were seen to Mrs A would lead Kitty around the, once grand, large entrance hall telling her about the various antique ornaments on the sideboards that lined two walls. Kitty knew them by heart as this was part of their daily routine, however to Mrs A, she was telling Kitty for the first time and so Kitty made the correct and expected responses during the tour. She was introduced to 'Lalique' and the pale pink vase that Mrs A was so fond of and which, sadly, was caked with years of dirt. Likewise, the precious Ming vase standing tall at the end of one sideboard.

Their next stop was the large drawing room which somehow had remained luxurious. Kitty imagined that the rest of the house must have been similarly kept at one time. It had beautiful furnishings with a large marble fireplace, adjacent to which was Mrs A's pride and joy, an exquisite inlaid antique dresser and the intricate cornicing and light roses completed the grandeur of the room.

Sadly, the rest of the house had been sorely neglected and the kitchen was not only unusable, but unsafe due to flood damage. This meant that Mrs A's meals were mainly ready made and heated in the microwave which, incongruously, was on a table at the foot of the grand staircase. Sometimes Kitty would bring some home made soup, which Mrs A relished.

Mrs A lived in her bedroom/sitting area with a bathroom accessed by an adjoining door, not to be confused with the modern 'en suite', and which was just as dilapidated as the rest of the house.

After their tour of Mrs A's treasures, Kitty drove her into Coldstream to the Co-op to shop for lunch. On Thursdays she took her to the post office as well, to collect her pension. Despite being very wealthy, Mrs A queued up patiently, signed for her money and gleefully put the cash into her purse.

Returning to the house Mrs A would run up the stairs, gazelle-like, then stop suddenly when she caught sight of her reflection in the large mirror on the landing half way up, she always remarked on how wrinkled she was and wondered when that had happened. Kitty attributed her fitness, at such an advanced age, to the fact that in Mrs A's mind, she was still a young woman with a young woman's litheness and energy.

Mrs A had a small ancient Ford pick-up which she was allowed to drive on the Estate. Her driving licence had been revoked when she was diagnosed with dementia and some afternoons she would drive Kitty around the Estate along the woodland tracks and visit the paddocks and stables that had once housed her horses. And so the routine of Mrs A and Kitty continued over the weeks and months of 2002.

THAT CHRISTMAS MRS A went to stay with friends on the west coast to celebrate the festive season. Kitty and Tommy's task now was to look after Pussy and they would take turns feeding her in the large garage at the foot of the back drive, which was her temporary home while the house was closed during Mrs A's absence.

It was around this time that Peter began to 'tag along', keenly exploring the grounds around Forestdean House. On discovering the garage, complete with 'pit', he asked Tommy if he could bring their old car, which had been off the road since they couldn't afford to tax it, his intention, he'd told Tommy, was to work on it and get it back on the road. Tommy agreed and so Peter went there whenever he felt like it.

Peter soon forgot about his intention to work on the car, as Kitty knew he would and growing bolder after searching around the outside of the big house, he had discovered an unlocked back door. Using this door since the rest of the house was securely locked, he explored the house from attic to basement and told Kitty about some of the things he'd found there. Feeling distinctly uneasy, Kitty told Peter that he shouldn't be going into the house while it was locked up and that he could get into trouble. He just laughed in her face and said that nobody would ever know ... unless she told them. He knew that Kitty would never do that because of her fear of the consequences.

Kitty was disappointed that Mrs A was away for longer than expected due to falling ill whilst staying with her friends. When she did return in the middle of January, she looked frail and poorly compared to how she'd been before Christmas. Her dementia was getting worse.

Jenny, Mrs A's niece who had Power of Attorney, had travelled from the south of England to assess the situation. On seeing that the dementia was advancing, she met with the consultant of the Geriatric Unit of the Borders General Hospital. He advised more intensive care in the interim, with possible admission to the Unit at some point in the not too distant future. Kitty and Tommy went to see Mrs A four times a day and, sadly, they could see that she was continuing to deteriorate.

Shortly after the new regime had been put in place, Kitty arrived one day to find Mrs A very disoriented and fretful. She called the geriatric unit, as previously advised, and was told to bring Mrs A in directly.

Kitty had to persuade Mrs A to go with her on 'an errand', as in her disoriented state she understandably wanted to remain at home. On arrival at the Unit she didn't want to leave the car. Kitty asked her again to come with her, saying she had to go in and pick something up at reception and, reluctantly, Mrs A finally agreed. Kitty left her in the waiting area while she spoke to the nurse in charge. The nurse told Kitty that she would take it from there and to leave without saying goodbye as that might upset the old lady further. Back in the car Kitty cried hot tears, she felt awful for luring Mrs A inside, although she knew she couldn't remain at home as she now needed care twenty-four hours a day.

Tommy called Kitty to say they were to continue their duties as they had when Mrs A was on holiday. Not long after this Tommy, instructed by Jenny, had CCTV and an alarm system installed at Forestdean House. Their new duties were, in addition to feeding Pussy, to monitor the CCTV footage daily and were given the code to set and disarm the alarm. Without Kitty knowing how he had managed it, Peter had appointed himself a member of the team. Kitty wasn't at all pleased and Tommy didn't seem unduly concerned.

Peter's first action was to take possession of the pick-up and use it as his own personal transport. Tommy didn't seem to mind so Kitty kept her own counsel despite worrying about Peter's motives regarding the big house.

Kitty's anxiety was proved to be well founded when Peter began to bring things home from Forestdean House. At first she thought he was just daft as she watched him offload hundreds of copies of 'The Times' newspapers from the pick-up. They had been piled up along the damp back corridors of the big house. For the sake of peace and personal safety, Kitty made no comment, even though, she asked herself the question 'why'?

She did, however, become seriously concerned when he

brought home the contents of the large kerosene tank (which was discreetly camouflaged on the back drive) in Jerry cans and stored them under the stairs. Apart from the fire risk, Kitty couldn't understand why he'd 'stolen' it since they had no use for it whatsoever. When she commented on it he said something about using it in the car so he wouldn't have to buy petrol. Totally mad, thought Kitty, but kept the thought to herself.

To Kitty, the worst time ever, she thought, was when he triumphantly presented her with a boxed set of antique crystal brandy goblets engraved with various country scenes. Kitty was shocked and told him to return them, they looked like they might have been heirlooms and they belonged in Forestdean House. With a bad grace he said,

"I thought you liked crystal brandy glasses, they'll not miss them." Kitty replied,

"I do like crystal brandy glasses, but not when they belong to someone else. Please Peter take them back." He took them away but whether he took them back or pawned them she neither knew nor asked.

However, worse was still to come. As Kitty parked the car in front of the big house one day, she saw the pickup there and knew, with a sinking heart, that Peter was around somewhere. The front door was wide open and she entered the house with trepidation. She could hardly believe the scene before her as she reached the back of the house and found him inside the walk-in safe, going through Mrs A's jewellery and other things which were kept there. He gleefully showed her boxes with necklaces, rings, bracelets, brooches etc. Kitty could hardly speak for the shock, when she did she said imploringly,

"Peter, for heavens sake come out of there! How on earth

did you get in anyway? I thought it was locked." He continued looking at the contents of the safe and said,

" It's okay, nobody will know and, anyway, I'm just looking." Kitty began to panic, worried that at any moment somebody would walk into the house and she would be implicated in his stupid, if not actually criminal, curiosity. Looking over her shoulder she urged him to come out and lock the door. Eventually, he did so.

That night Kitty phoned Tommy and said she wasn't coming back. She made the excuse that the job wasn't the same without Mrs A and that there really wasn't enough work for three of them. The truth was that she didn't want to be caught up in Peter's nefarious activities.

IN FEBRUARY 2003 they moved yet again, to another of the Estate's properties. This time it was to a remote lodge house. Kitty was now totally socially and geographically isolated. She didn't have work as respite and she was far from the nearest neighbours deep within the woodland of the Estate.

Peter's already strange behaviour was becoming quite ... bizarre ... yes that was the only word to describe it, Kitty mused one day. Heck, she thought, strange, bizarre, whatever was becoming the order of the day. Being reasonably close to Kelso, Peter became obsessed with the Sunday Market there where traders from up and down the country came and set up their stalls, which were many and varied. Kitty took the opportunity to buy fruit and vegetables at prices which easily beat the local supermarket.

However, it was the Tool Man, a moniker Kitty had given him, that Peter seemed most interested in. Each Sunday while Kitty walked around the various stalls and bought the weekly fruit and vegetables, Peter hung around Frank's gazebo inspecting his impressive display of multifarious tools, screws, nuts and bolts for sale. He never left without buying a substantial amount.

Over the weeks and months he had bought enough DIY paraphernalia to be start his own Sunday stall. He never used any of these purchases to improve the lodge house, instead, he drove rows of long nails into the walls of the large garage on which he hung the tools, packets of nails etc. Amused, Kitty thought that it looked like a DIY exhibition. In addition to the main garage, the lodge had a large wooden garage and Peter managed to fill both with what Kitty regarded as 'junk'. There was no room for the car, which froze outside during winter. There was an adjoining building which had obviously been dog kennels and they thought the lodge had once housed a game-keeper. Before finally leaving the lodge, those same kennels would be found to house its most unusual items ever.

One Saturday, on their monthly visit, Kitty showed her sisters Peter's tool 'exhibition'. She smiled at their bemused expressions and said,

"Don't ask me, I just live here and you can see for your-selves by the state of the house, that he's not using them there!" Just as they were leaving, they noticed a chair bearing a tag with Mrs A's late husband's name on it and 'ER' on the chair back. She told her sisters that she hadn't seen it before and guessed Peter must have taken it from Forestdean House. She remembered Mrs A mentioning that her husband had been invited to the Queen's Coronation.

In the summer of that year Mrs A's niece, Jenny, put Forestdean House on the market and Peter was redundant. This was bad news for Kitty since it meant he was at home all the time. At least, she thought consolingly, she wasn't worrying about what he might be stealing from Mrs A's house.

Peter's behaviour towards Kitty worsened at the lodge, playing mind games and testing her often. She came back from a solitary walk in the fields one day to find a rope hanging from the back of the garage. He told Kitty that he was going to hang himself and waited for Kitty's reaction. She didn't know what to say, since whatever she said would be the wrong response. She tried to side-step it, but was unsuccessful and he raged,

"You want me dead, don't you?" Kitty protested, but secretly knew the answer was 'yes'. Her life with Peter was a miserable rollercoaster and she desperately wanted to get off it without falling from a great height herself. She didn't know how to stop the awful, seemingly perpetual, motion without killing him herself. She was terrified she might slip 'over the edge' and be driven to stabbing him in his sleep and what the judicial consequences of that would be. She had heard of women who had and one prison was substituted for another. No, she must at all costs, avoid toppling over. She must get away from Peter for the sake of her sanity, her life and possibly her freedom.

Towards the end of 2003, Kitty began to think that the only hope she had of being free of Peter was if they returned to Edinburgh where there were services and support that would help her to get away and stay away - safely. She realised that living in the lodge she was too far from the help she needed. Just before Christmas Peter had been informed that his additional benefit was to stop in January as it had been decided at his last mental health assessment that he no longer needed it. He was very angry that this extra 'easy money' was to be withdrawn and said to Kitty that he would have to look for work since the basic benefit wasn't nearly enough for his needs. Kitty thought to herself, yes *his* needs including keeping the Tool Man in business!

At Christmas Peter decided to visit his parents whom he had become estranged from over some perceived slight or other. She thought his real motive was to check out the work situation whilst having free food and accommodation close to Edinburgh. Kitty encouraged the visit and said he should stay for two weeks, but in the end, he stayed away for only one. Nevertheless during that time, she called agencies in Edinburgh for advice and she then devised a plan of action to leave Peter as early as possible in the New Year.

In January 2004, Kitty talked lightly to Peter about new year resolutions and said she remembered him talking about going back to Edinburgh since there were more work opportunities there than in the Borders, now that his extra money had been stopped. To her huge relief he agreed, believing it to be his own idea. They started looking for affordable flats in Edinburgh, but it took them until early spring to find suitable accommodation.

POSTSCRIPT

When the factor of the Estate came to check on the newly vacated lodge house and outbuildings he found in the kennels what appeared to be lots of squares of metal with sharp edges. He scratched his head wondering where on earth they came from and it wasn't until he had removed most of it and discovered an engine, that he realised the pieces of metal had once been a car.

Rather than pay for it to be legally scrapped, over the weeks before finding the Edinburgh flat Peter had painstakingly dismantled the old car and cut it up with a grinder from Frank's stall, having first removed the engine.

7

EDINBURGH 2005

One year ago, Kitty had finally left Peter for good, not without drama, and had settled into a large sunny room in a house in a fashionable part of Edinburgh. This had been home since leaving Peter, she would have preferred a flat but, at the moment, the room was affordable and, being south facing, was bright. She had added her own bits and pieces to the basic furniture which was there when she had moved into the furnished let and it had a tasteful, feminine feel to it. She relished the freedom to make the room her own in a way she had never been able to do with Peter. Apart from not having enough money to make their home comfortable, there was always the danger that he would wreck anything she cherished in a vindictive temper. She appreciated her own space, made comfortable by her little personal and stylish touches.

She was reasonably content there but there were still feelings about those years with Peter that niggled at her and stopped her having complete peace of mind. The questions she couldn't answer satisfactorily and which kept going round and around in her head were: What *had* happened to her?; How had she gone from being a free woman to a virtual hostage in a relatively short space of time? Those questions were at the forefront of her mind that Thursday evening, having made the decision to see a therapist. She wanted, no she needed to recover, or perhaps rediscover, the old Kitty. She wanted her former self back. She wanted to feel again that zest for life that so many years ago had taken her on a world backpacking trip as a solo traveller. She knew she had to be in therapy to recover from the damage that being married to Peter had done and to be totally free of him mentally and emotionally. It would be a hard and probably painful journey, but she knew she definitely had to get off the continual and relentless merry-go-round of self-blame. Her first appointment had been arranged for the following morning.

As she sat in the bay window of her comfy room and looked out at the purple and orange-tinged, darkening sky, she wondered what to expect. Would she have to tell the story in all its gory detail? She shuddered at this prospect. She couldn't visualise herself telling a complete stranger about the awful and varied experiences she had suffered. Before she could stop herself, some of the incidents started running through her mind as though she was watching a film. The time he had put his hands around her neck and squeezed, it seemed to have happened out of the blue. She remembered thinking that she was dreaming and in the dream she was calling for Peter to help her. Only it wasn't a dream, it was actually happening. The 'dream' part, she realised afterwards, was when she had lost consciousness for however long he had been squeezing her throat. There had been no argument, just his displeasure when he saw the two empty wine glasses on the table when he had come home from his shift in the taxi. Her friend Charles had dropped by with a bottle of wine and a housewarming present. Peter hated Charles as much as he hated Kitty enjoying a glass of wine with her friend. He had suddenly lost his temper and throttled Kitty to teach her a lesson.

Over time his sudden changes of mood had her walking on eggshells for fear of setting him off. She became very attuned to the undercurrent of the threat of violence and she would go into 'appeasement mode' in order to avoid some 'punishment' or other. It rarely worked if he was intent on hurting or terrorising her. He enjoyed the feeling of power he got from being able to frighten her. He was not necessarily going to carry out the threat, but he wanted her to know he *could*.

The film was now playing the horrific scenes from the aftermath of the prostitute incident. Returning from a late shift, he could see she had been crying. Rather than comfort her, he flew into an almighty rage. She had been sitting at one end of the sofa when he picked up a large kitchen knife and repeatedly stabbed it into the cushion next to her head. Terrified, she had covered her face with her hands in the hope of protecting herself. He suddenly changed tactics and attempted to squeeze her throat. It must be true what they say about people finding an unusual strength in life or death situations because she was able to prise his fingers from her throat. The next thing she was aware of was a searing pain in one of her fingers - he was biting it as hard as he could. A visit to the A&E next day confirmed he had broken it.

With great effort of will she stopped the 'video'. She decided all aspects of her story, from being afraid to voice her opinions, the violence, the abject poverty, his foray into pornography, the constant and continual sabotage of her plans would probably be told over the duration of her time in therapy.

It wasn't surprising that Kitty had a restless sleep with dreams about the past and wakeful wondering as to what the morning would bring. She eventually fell into a light sleep around 5.30am.

8

"THE JOURNEY BEGINS"

Kitty was wakened by her alarm at 7.30 next morning and, rolling onto her side, quickly turned it off so as not to disturb anyone else in the house. She lay on her back gathering her thoughts. The sun-dappled leaves on the silver birch outside her window cast a green and gold shadow upon the wall and ceiling above her head. She loved spring and she left her curtains open so she could watch the play of light and shadow in the room in the mornings, deriving a sense of calm from the gentle movement. She mused that spring was a time of new beginnings and hoped this was auspicious for what she was about to embark upon. As she watched the shadow-dance, she contemplated the day ahead and her eleven o'clock appointment in particular. She felt both relief and dread as she thought about it. Relief that she had made the decision to seek professional help and dread of what it might entail. Shaking herself mentally, she got out of bed and headed for the communal bathroom to start the day with a shower.

. . .

SHE SAT ALONE in the waiting room of the Cedar Tree Therapy Centre in the Morningside area of Edinburgh. She had chosen this particular service because it offered therapists who were trained to work specifically with the kind of trauma she had suffered and the issues she was facing as a result. She had dressed carefully for this appointment and wore her favourite long, floaty skirt in blue and purple tones which always gave her a sense of calm. Her jacket was cobalt blue and seemed to lend some colour to her once bright eyes. Her hair, which framed her delicately-boned features, added a look of serenity which she certainly did not feel.

Suddenly, she was aware of another person in the room as a man asked gently,

"Kitty Dawson?" She started from her reverie and stood up quickly, collecting her bag as she did so.

"Hello, I'm Nick Jones, good morning!" He said offering her his outstretched hand to shake hers.

"Please come through." He led her along a short corridor into one of the counselling rooms with a sign on the door which read 'Do Not Disturb, Session in Progress'. He indicated a chair where she should sit and then seated himself. The room was comfortable and had the soft lighting of table lamps. The chairs, carpet and walls were in neutral colours and there were pastel prints on the walls. The table next to her chair held a glass of water and a box of tissues. It was a room, Kitty reflected, to put a person at ease, or as much at ease as one could be at a first therapy session.

When she appeared to be comfortable Nick explained about confidentiality, duration of sessions and the therapy contract in general. In other words, they agreed to a course of work together. He then asked,

"What is it you hope to gain from this particular kind of therapy work?" Kitty chewed her lower lip, this was a question she had been mulling over for some time. She took a deep breath and said falteringly,

"I'm hoping ... to make sense of ... what has been happening in my life ... these past years ... and to get back to being the person I used to be." She sighed at having said this much. "It's hard to know where to start" she paused, trying to find the right words, "it happened over several years and wasn't just one thing but many, or maybe the same thing happened repeatedly but in different ways." This came out in a rush and she looked at the therapist apologetically, thinking that what she had just said sounded totally nonsensical. His next words reassured her that he had understood. He said,

"It's okay Kitty, we have plenty of time to work on this, so just take your time. It may be easier for you if you begin by telling me what it is that's troubling you most at this moment and then we can take it from there." That's easy, she thought and said,

"The worst part of the whole horrible situation is that I feel it's all my fault, that I allowed it to happen. I should have done something to stop it. I should have got out, left, gone far away, something, anything ... but I felt powerless to make decisions or do anything, so I stayed." She was crying freely now, big round tears of shame and guilt for having been so powerless, trapped in a relationship with a violent and controlling man. When she had calmed down she said, sounding somewhat confused, "But I was so afraid to leave, even when he stood holding the door wide open, almost taunting me to go. I was terrified to step over the threshold, the underlying menace and threat of violence, or worse, were palpable."

Nick Jones was an experienced therapist working with survivors of domestic abuse who eventually managed to escape violent and controlling situations. These women were emotionally and psychologically scarred due to the long term duration and repetition of the abuse and needed specialised help to recover and begin to live meaningful lives again. In his late forties, Nick was dark haired with an open, friendly face and had crinkly laughter lines around his kind, dark brown eyes. He was the kind of person whose innate sense of calm would induce others to trust him. He looked kindly at Kitty and said,

"It's really important Kitty for you to know and remember that you are not to blame for someone else's bad behaviour and violence towards you." He looked at her as his words sunk in. She sighed and said,

"But I should have left or gone to the police. That's what some people would say." She shook her head and continued, "No, I was too scared to go to the police, they couldn't protect me twenty-four hours a day." Nick agreed saying,

"No and you have also told me that you were afraid to leave, so was it really an option for you?" She thought about this for a moment and said,

"No you're right, and besides, he kept telling me that I could run but I couldn't hide - the fear was paralysing. Sometimes I would be on the brink of doing something dangerous to get myself away from his threats."

"Can you tell me a bit more about that Kitty?" Nick asked looking concerned.

"Once, when he was supposed to be giving me a lift to work, he drove in the opposite direction and we were travelling along a deserted, little used country road. As I said earlier, at those times the threat was so strong I could almost smell it. Feeling the sheer terror of what might have lain ahead, I undid the seatbelt and was about to jump from the moving car. He stopped the car, shouting at me to stop being so stupid, but turned in the direction we should have been going. I could sense his enjoyment at being able to instil such fear in me." After a few moments silence Nick then said,

"It must have taken a lot of courage to finally leave, given how afraid you were. How did you do that?" Kitty thought before replying,

"You know, the time when it worked, that last time when I finally got away, wasn't that difficult. It was all the other times, the failed attempts for one reason or another that were so hard and draining. I made a complete break from him last spring after a serious attack on me. I remember, in January of last year, I made myself a promise that that year would be different. I was going to be fifty in June and I knew in my bones if I didn't change what was happening, I would be trapped for the rest of my life. I just kept saying to myself that at this stage of my life, things should be getting easier, not more difficult." Nick glanced at the clock and said,

"We're just about out of time Kitty." She continued as though she hadn't heard him, saying,

"Do you know, the funny thing is that when I first met him I didn't like him at all. I thought he was forward, presumptuous and altogether too familiar. Why did I not listen to my gut instinct? Why did I get entangled with him later?" Nick replied,

"That sounds like a good place to start next week Kitty. Same time next Friday?" She nodded, gathering up her bag and stuffing sodden hankies into it. He left her in the waiting room and said,

"Go well, I'll see you next week."

9

"REFLECTIONS"

Once outside the Centre, Kitty drew a deep refreshing breath. Edinburgh is particularly lovely in spring with cherry and apple blossom-covered trees. Despite being a busy city there still remained many tree-lined streets, especially in this part of Edinburgh where the houses were detached Victorian villas set well back from the road. Most had long driveways with large secluded gardens to the rear.

Kitty thought that it was too lovely a day to go back to her room in the quiet house and decided to go to Portobello and walk along the Promenade to reflect on her session with Nick and the memories it had triggered. As she reached the bus stop, a number 5 Lothian Region bus was arriving, which was lucky as it meant she didn't have to change buses in Princes Street. Thirty minutes later she alighted near the west end of Portobello Promenade and she began her walk along the waterfront towards Joppa, on the city's north eastern boundary.

As she ambled along, she thought again about her first impression of Peter Parnell and how that encounter had come about. She had been officiating at an athletics meeting and he had been competing in some event or other. She didn't know what, although she had seen him around the sports centre before. As he walked by he made a remark, she couldn't remember what but knew it had been inappropriate. Yes, that's what had struck her at the time so she hadn't deigned to respond. He had wanted her to notice him. She was certain now that her first impression of him had been correct, so where and why had she gone wrong and become enmeshed with such a man? To answer that question she would have to go back to the time before she had become involved with him - the time of travel and discovery.

IN 1992 KITTY made a life changing decision. She had always wanted to travel, to see places and sights she had only ever read about or had seen on television. She had read 'Feel the Fear and Do It Anyway' and had asked herself, why wait until retirement to travel? Why not do it now while she still had her health and sense of adventure? An important factor in making this decision was her friend Lois, who lived in Syracuse in up-state New York. Lois was forty-one years old and had terminal cancer. This galvanised Kitty into action. She put her flat up for sale and planned a trip around the world on the proceeds. The flat sold quickly and she resigned from her job with the local council. She set out to travel the world, or as much of it as her multi-stop ticket allowed. Unlike many travellers at the time, Kitty's route went from east to west and she began her journey in America.

The reason for this was simple. Kitty wanted to see Lois before she died and wouldn't risk missing her friend by going the conventional backpacker west to east route. Her adventure started by reconnecting with Boston, a favourite of hers and one of the oldest cities in the United States, dating back to 1630. Situated on the Charles River, it comprised both old and new architecture. She particularly loved the massive under-cover Faneuil Hall market with its plethora of eating places, clothing and jewellery outlets; a veritable shoppers' paradise. There, she met up with an old friend and colleague before hurrying off to Cape Cod and a whale watching trip. From Boston Kitty travelled to Connecticut and spent several enjoyable days with friends she'd had as a teenager in Edinburgh and who had emigrated to New England twenty years previously. The identical twin sisters and their older brother played in a band and Kitty had the unexpected pleasure of joining them on stage, at a society wedding gig they were doing in a country club in Greenwich Village. Kitty played tambourine and she had a ball with her old pals. Other places visited by Kitty in the States are too numerous to mention, however she spent four weeks in Syracuse which gave her time to spend with Lois who was in hospital and very poorly. Kitty sent Lois postcards from every destination and dedicated her tandem skydive over Lake Taupo, in New Zealand, to her friend just weeks before she died.

In retrospect, and ironically noting that hindsight is 20:20, Kitty particularly recalled her travels in New Zealand, where she gravitated to New Age people, shops, books and workshops. She learned about karma, auras and unconditional love and the latter, she now observed, had been at the root of her future downfall with Peter Parnell. She had been totally unaware of the vulnerability that this path would lead her to.

At this point in her reminiscences she stopped to sit on a bench looking out over the Firth of Forth, towards where she thought Kinghorn lay in the hazy distance. As she gazed over the calm waters of the River Forth, she began to wonder if she had been on another planet back then. No, she decided ... or maybe yes, since she had been so far removed, not only geographically, but from the 'real world' she had left behind in Edinburgh. She smiled as she recollected Anna, the most cautious of her sisters, sounding horrified and asking where she would live on her return, since she had sold her home. Kitty replied simply that it was 'only four walls and a roof' and that she would find somewhere. She also recalled the feeling of freedom from having to worry, or at least deal with, things like mortgage payments, council tax, utilities etc and the phrase 'trappings of wealth' which had come to mind often during her trip. As the youngest of six children, Kitty had always felt 'different', perhaps as a baby she'd been given to the wrong mother after she was born? However, the strong resemblance between siblings negated this fancy. She was the only one to 'stay on' at school and later get a university degree.

She stood up and carried on along the promenade as she continued her reflections of her world tour, the act of walking seemed to lend momentum to her thoughts. She clearly remembered saying to a friend that she would know by the end of her travels what it was she wanted to do with her life, so it was also to be a journey of self-discovery. She realised it wasn't the many wonderful sights she had seen or the interesting people she had met in such far away places; it was her emotional and psychological outlook - how she viewed the world - that had travelled the most distance. It was precisely that simultaneous 'other trip' that had her questioning which planet she had been on at that time. The basic massage workshop and introduction to 'subtle energies' she had been on that memorable weekend in New

Zealand, was definitely a factor in her ideas crystallising into a plan her life might take on her return home. She suddenly remembered the saying *travel broadens the mind*.

Kitty recollected how, after nine months of travel, she had gone back to Edinburgh happy, optimistic and enthusiastic about everything. Within two days she had secured a job back in the office where she had worked before going overseas and a week later had found a room in a shared flat in the lovely Inverleith district of Edinburgh, close to the Royal Botanical Gardens. She had spent many happy hours walking there, contemplating what she would do next. Then one day in September, she believed the Universe had smiled on her when she received a letter from her massage tutor in New Zealand, inviting her to take a place at the newly established New Zealand College of Massage and to be one of the first students to study there the following February. Kitty jumped at this opportunity and believed that the money to finance the trip would materialise if it was meant to be.

Kitty concentrated her efforts on making enough money to travel there to do the diploma course. As it transpired, money came pouring in from a variety of sources providing sufficient funds for travel, fees and living expenses whilst studying in Auckland. To Kitty this was proof that, with the blessing of the Universe, she was embarking on a predestined new phase of what she believed was sure to be a wonderful life.

10

"HINDSIGHT IS 20:20"

A t her next therapy session Kitty told Nick how she came to be involved with Peter Parnell. She continued with her account,

"It was about three months before I was due to leave for New Zealand and I got a phone call from him asking if I would like to meet for a drink and chat as he'd heard I was going away again - the sports centre is a great source of news for its regulars. I was rather surprised as the last time I saw him, in passing at the Centre, he had been very dismissive, as though I was the last person he wanted to talk to. At the time, I felt he had engaged with me just so he could reject me, perhaps he had picked up my strong feelings of dislike for him. However I agreed, wondering why the sudden interest?" Surprised Nick asked,

"Do you know why you agreed to meet a man who was so rude to you?" Kitty replied,

"I suppose it was to do with my way of looking at people at the time ... I thought maybe he was feeling bad about the way he had spoken to me at the sports centre and I decided to give him the benefit of my, previously considerable, doubts. Also, I thought people deserved second chances and, anyway, what harm could it do when I was going away soon?" Nick looked at her thoughtfully, as though he could see the harm, but said nothing. Kitty went on,

"We met one Sunday evening in a hotel in Princes Street, it was a favourite of mine as it overlooked the floodlit Gardens and the Scott Monument. The hotel was cosy and had a relaxed atmosphere conducive to conversation. Peter was clean-shaven, tidier than I had seen him before. He was wearing a leather jacket and altogether he looked as though he had made an effort to clean up. I had only ever seen him in track suits and training gear and he always had a rather grubby appearance. He showed an interest in what I had been doing and what I was planning to do, which was a complete turnaround from the last conversation we had."

"You were surprised by this new interest in your life?" Nick asked. Kitty replied,

"I was ... I couldn't quite match up the two different Peters ... I thought I might have misjudged him before." Nick then asked Kitty,

"In what way did he seem different? What was it that changed your opinion of him, as you clearly had?" Kitty pondered this question and then said,

"He seemed more mature than previous encounters, you know, not the cocksure guy who enjoyed having an audience of the lads. I suppose he was serious rather than playing the fool. He came across as being considerate and thoughtful."

"What do you think had brought about this change in his ... personality, shall we call it?" Asked Nick. Kitty suddenly retorted,

"Of course I know now that there hadn't been any change from the smart-arsed, crude oaf he had originally presented as!" A dark flush of anger spread upwards from her neck. Nick said gently,

"Kitty don't beat yourself up, save your anger for Peter." She lifted the glass of water from the table with a shaky hand and took a sip to give herself time to calm down.

"No, you're right" she said after a few moments, "and I'm digressing from trying to explain how and why I was taken in by him." She took a deep breath and began to tell Nick how, over a period of three months, he had charmed her. He had talked about politics and history and was interested in everything she had to say. He was impressed by her academic achievements and had told her his (sad) story of being railroaded into an apprenticeship at a local construction firm and how his parents had never taken any interest in their only child's badminton competitions. This had immediately aroused her sympathy. Continuing with her account Kitty said,

"Just days before I left for Auckland, he told me that he loved me and didn't want me to go. He said that anyone who had been important in his life or he had trusted, had left him, abandoned him." Nick asked,

"How did you feel when he said that, when he put such an emotional load onto you?" Kitty said,

"I was flattered, but it wasn't going to change my plans." She thought for a moment then said,

"No, I was enough 'me' then. I told him he could write to me, that we could keep in touch by letter. I left Edinburgh early in February and stopped in San Francisco to visit family and to break up such a long journey. The course exceeded my expectations and I learned so much. The other students were very friendly and I even found a part time job to supplement my funds." Nick then asked,

"Did Peter write to you?" Shaking her head Kitty replied,

"No he didn't, not until after I had phoned a friend in Edinburgh and asked him to make sure he was okay. I don't know why I even bothered and subsequently wished I hadn't "

She told Nick of how she had received only one badly written letter in all the time she was there. She said that she had developed a close friendship with a woman on the course. Kathy was a bit older than her and was originally from Liverpool and they got on well. Kitty had spent a lot of time with her, both socially and as 'study buddies'. She had met Kathy's husband and family and had stayed over some weekends. She trusted Kathy and, over the months, had talked to her about Peter and how he seemed to have an 'out of sight, out of mind' attitude. She expressed her view to Kathy that a friendship, let alone a relationship, if that's what she'd had with Peter, was a two-way street and she wasn't investing any more than she already had. It would be madness to keep giving when nothing was coming back. No, she had decided, she would no longer put up with 'diminishing returns' on her energy and emotional investment in Peter Parnell. Kitty said that she actually felt relieved when she had made this decision ... then Kathy suggested she give him a second chance.

"It's interesting" she reflected, "that once I had let go emotionally, he was the one to make contact. It was as if some psychic message had winged its way to him from across the world. He phoned me and told me how much he missed me and how he was looking forward to my return in a few weeks time."

"How did you feel about that?" Nick asked. Kitty replied,

"Well I had been feeling really good since deciding enough was enough and I wasn't impressed or flattered. Now that I had my Diploma in Therapeutic Massage and there was no possibility of me remaining in New Zealand because of visa restrictions, I was looking forward to seeing family and friends again and setting up in massage therapy. If it had been at all possible, I would have stayed there. I loved the country and the friendly and generous 'Kiwis'. How I wished so many times over these past years, that I had not come home. If I had known the terror and tyranny that would blight my life, I would have remained there, even without a valid visa. I fantasised often, especially in the darkest hours, about having stayed and married a kind New Zealand man and living happily ever after, or at least, happier and safer than I was when trapped by Peter Parnell." Nick said,

"Kitty if we all had the benefit of hindsight we would make very different decisions. As it stands, it's only with the clarity of time passing and our experiences that hindsight is what it is: looking back." Kitty thought about Nick's words for a few moments then said,

"You're absolutely right Nick. I'm now thinking back to when he picked me up at the airport and the conversation we had in a café we stopped at on the way home. Peter said that he was glad I was back because he missed me and I remember thinking *you missed me so much you wrote just one lousy letter.* I replied that a lot of people missed me and I was looking forward to seeing them again. This obviously didn't please him as he said that he didn't care about other people, he 'needed me'." Nick asked Kitty,

"What did you make of that at the time?" After a thoughtful moment she said,

"At the time I thought he was being childish and rather selfish, but now I know it was more than childishness. I believe that I was still very much the self-contained 'me' and he wanted sole possession of me. I had no idea then what that would come to mean." Looking at the clock Nick said,

"We have to stop there for today Kitty, same time next week?" Kitty nodded, thanked him and made her way out of the Centre.

11

"A VALLEY DARK WITH FEAR"

The dream was a recurring one and it was always the same with the panic and fear almost paralysing her. She was desperately trying to shut the door and every time she pushed it to, the latch would not click into place and the door would not stay closed. She pushed and pushed as her terror intensified, knowing there was danger on the other side pushing against her, something ... someone ... much stronger than her. Suddenly she wakened with a thud. Sweat was pouring from her and her heart was pounding like kettle drums in her ears. Her breathing was so laboured she felt like she had just finished a hundred metres sprint.

Kitty switched on her bedside lamp and looked at the clock, it was 2am. The terror had subsided somewhat on seeing the familiar surroundings, but she still felt fearful. Once her heart rate had calmed a bit, she lay listening. There was only silence. She felt reassured being in a house with other people and her bedroom door had been fitted with a deadlock. Although during her waking hours she was no longer afraid of Peter, when she woke from the recurring dream she felt the old fears that Peter would track her down and charm one of the other tenants to let him into the building. She felt it difficult to repel such irrational fears during the 'graveyard hours' when things always felt at their worst; whether it was frightening dreams or the everyday worries that most people experience more acutely at that time of night.

In that not quite awake state and before she could shake off the feelings of fear, the flashbacks began. Images of his violence and his threats of killing her came unbidden, playing before her open eyes like a video recording. Shaking her head, she tried to rid herself of the picture of him pinning her to the sofa, hands tight around her throat, snarling 'die bitch', flecks of spittle spattering her face.

THERE WAS NO GOING BACK to sleep, at least not for an hour or so, she decided to make herself a cup of tea. She was glad she had filled the kettle earlier as she was reluctant to leave the safety of her room. While she waited for the kettle to boil she closed the bedroom curtains and peeped between them, making sure the street was quiet and nobody was lingering in the shadows, grateful that she had an upstairs room. She sat in the only armchair, cradling a mug of tea in her hands, asking herself the question she had asked a thousand times. Why didn't she leave? She had left, many times but had gone back. Why? She was hoping to find the answers during her course of therapy. She remembered the Women's Aid worker telling her not to beat herself up for going back, it often took ten or more attempts before a woman was able to finally leave an abusive husband, the reasons for this were many and complex. Okay Kitty, she told herself, put the stick away for now.

Thinking of this, her mind turned to her 'Great Escapes' and she smiled ruefully at the two which might reasonably fall into this category. Both were serious attempts to go far enough away so she would not be tempted to go back the same day. The first 'flight' was to a friend in London. This was after the 'die bitch' incident, which happened not long after he had told her he'd had sex with a prostitute he had picked up in Leith, an area well known for the trade. Kitty was so shocked and hurt, especially so since he disapproved of people cheating on their spouses and partners, it was the last thing she expected of him. He had totally betrayed her trust. What made it more painful was telling her on her, then favourite beach, rubbing salt into the wound he'd just inflicted on her. At the time she had thought the attack had come out of the blue, but she now wondered whether it was his perverse way of avoiding feeling guilty when he saw how hurt she still was. This made it her fault, or as he often accused her, "you made me do it".

The other escape was to the Outer Hebrides, there was no going home from there the same day, she smiled as she recalled the long, lonely journey. This came about due to a distinct but tacit threat of violence which occurred one morning, just as she was leaving for work. The job at the time was another of his decisions for her. It was safer to comply with his plans, so she became a taxi driver and worked similar shifts to his. That way she would be available to be his personal trainer, which she knew she was not qualified to do. This was another of his schemes to 'be someone', to be the famous Peter Parnell star of the world badminton scene. He'd said she was his 'superwoman', the one who would help him realise his dreams. Inevitably she had failed as had all the other significant women in his life, the first being his mother. Thinking about it now, he was clearly displaying misogynistic tendencies: all women would pay for his mother's neglect. The physical violence was not so frequent at times, it was more the threat of it. When was it going to happen? What form would it take? The 'sword of Damocles' constantly hovered above her head. On this occasion she was about to leave the house when she felt the strong, dark undercurrent of danger which always gave her a sick feeling in the pit of her stomach, almost rooting her to the floor with fear. She quickly picked up the car keys and left the flat, her heart racing. She didn't go to work that day, instead she went to Women's Aid where she spoke to a very understanding woman who arranged for her to travel to their Stornaway refuge the next day. Kitty was in such a state of panic, the woman did everything for her; booking her seat on the bus, her ferry tickets and a place in the refuge. She stayed with her sister Denise and Peter wouldn't know why she hadn't come home that night. The next day he would get the car keys in the post with instructions on where to find it.

As she finished her now cold tea, Kitty acknowledged that those weren't realistic attempts to leave. They did however separate her from actual and potentially violent situations, for the duration at least. They were also, in her own way, acts of defiance. Just thinking that brought an awareness that a kernel of her former self must have been there still, deep inside, like a tiny pilot light waiting to be ignited again. Much calmer now, Kitty felt sleepy enough to return to bed although she knew she would sleep fitfully as was usual after such dreams. She had to get up for work in the morning and be the complementary health care worker with a smile on her face. Sometimes she felt such a fraud, trying to help other people when she needed help herself. Then she reminded herself, that was why she was in therapy.

12

"HIS DARK CLOUD EVER HOVERS

THEN VIOLENTLY BURSTS."

A t her next session Kitty told Nick about the recurring dream and its aftermath of flashbacks, running like a video in front of her eyes. Nick observed,

"What you are telling me through this dream is that you are still deeply traumatised by your experience of living with abuse over a number of years, hence the recurring dream. Your fear of Peter still exists deep in your subconscious mind. Kitty, have you heard of 'PTSD', post traumatic stress disorder?" Asked Nick, she replied,

"Yes, isn't that when someone has trouble getting over an event like a car crash?" Nick nodded and said,

"That's one kind." He then explained, "there are two types of post traumatic stress disorder: type 1 is caused by a single event which is perceived by the person as traumatic. The other type, the kind you experienced, happens when someone is subjected to repeated trauma or abuse over a period of time. This is known as Complex Trauma and requires specialised help to recover from it. The crucial factor for recovery is that you are in a safe place where you can begin to heal and rebuild your life. You have managed to find a room in a house where you feel safe and you have started to reconstruct your life. However, the damage that Peter inflicted, so often and so insidiously, will take time to recover from. The fact that you are coming here means you know that something more than just time is necessary; it's the intensive work undertaken in therapy which drives the healing process." Kitty sat in silence taking this in then said,

"So what you are saying is that I was locked in that situation by the repeated incidents of violence, threats and fear? Even the thought of getting away ... away properly I mean ... seemed so fraught with difficulties. I didn't have the mental or physical energy to try ... or the courage. I remember one of the times he held the door open, telling me to go and I just froze, like a rabbit caught in headlights." Suddenly realisation dawned on Kitty. "That's why I found it so hard to leave? In addition, I had no money to support myself." Nick nodded and said,

"Leaving an abusive relationship is difficult for many reasons. Abused women have lost everything they had before the relationship: their confidence; their sense of self; freedom to be with family and friends or to make their own decisions; financial independence, all are systematically taken away from them. Their world shrinks considerably until it is literally and emotionally confined to the relationship and the coercive control of their partner." While Nick was talking Kitty was nodding recognition of herself in this description.

"Yes, I can see how that happened to me and we moved house so often too that I couldn't put down any roots or make friends." Nick asked,

"Who initiated the moves Kitty?" She replied without hesitation,

"Him of course, everything had to be what and when he wanted." She sighed, "we moved house about every six months, always further and further away from Edinburgh, family and friends. Eventually, we were in a lodge house in a remote part of a country estate, far from the nearest neighbours and certainly out of hearing distance of cries for help." Kitty shuddered at the thought of the remote house, then laughing ironically she said, "actually, it was a family joke, my sister Anna began writing my latest address in pencil so she could rub it out and put the next one in." Tears formed in her eyes and Nick asked gently,

"What is it you are feeling right now Kitty?" As the tears streamed silently down her face she said,

"No one would have understood the isolation I felt, not just living in a house far from others and help, but the isolation of the 'secret'."

"Tell me about the secret Kitty." Nick said gently, she replied,

"My life was the secret. I hid the true nature of it from everyone. I couldn't tell anyone what my marriage to Peter was really like. My sisters had no idea of the kind of life I was living, if it could be called that, and I couldn't tell them. I felt so ashamed of ending up like that." Crying properly and with a hint of anger, she continued, "I also had some stupid sense of loyalty to him, I didn't want my family to think badly of him. How stupid is that?" Nick replied,

"It wasn't stupid at all Kitty, in fact it was instinctive self-preservation. What do you think would have happened if you had told them?" She said more calmly now,

"I was so afraid of his anger that I didn't even contemplate telling them, all hell would have broken loose! You know, now that I'm voicing it to you, I don't think I would have had the words to tell it back then." Nick then said, referring to something Kitty had said earlier,

"I didn't know you had sisters, you haven't mentioned them before." She smiled somewhat ruefully and said,

"Yes, I have three sisters and they were *allowed* to visit once a month. I looked forward to the respite." Nick regarded her quizzically and Kitty said,

"He was Mr Charm himself during their visits and they took me for lunch which was a great treat. They always brought gifts, usually their unwanted clothes or bits and pieces for the house, which I gratefully accepted." Nick looking confused now asked,

"I'm sorry Kitty but I thought Peter was a taxi driver, was he out of work then?" Kitty sighed,

"We lived in abject poverty for years. When his Commonwealth Games dreams died he rented a taxi full time, but he rarely worked full time. About six months after moving to the country, he got himself diagnosed with depression and was on benefits, at least the rent and council tax got paid on time then. Before then there were times when he wouldn't go to work for days on end and by the end of the week the rental fee was often more than his takings. The result was poverty and debt. The inside of our home spoke volumes, no floor coverings other than the odd rug and not enough curtains for all the windows. I gave up my part time job as every pound I earned came off his sickness benefit and life was bad enough without walking three miles to work and back for nothing." In answer to Nick's questioning look she said,

"The car was off the road because we couldn't tax and MOT it and there was one bus a day from where we were living to the town where I worked." Kitty paused there, remembering. Nick just nodded, indicating she should go on. "You can see how I loved my sisters' visits, it was like a window to the outside world where life was normal and sane and colourful." She nodded sadly, "It was a mono-chrome existence in many ways. When they left and I waved them goodbye, the sun that had been shining all day suddenly disappeared behind a dark cloud."

Nick was looking thoughtful and said,

"You have covered a lot of ground today Kitty, do you feel you are starting to put the pieces together? What I mean is, are you beginning to understand how you were coerced into and trapped in that situation?" Kitty replied,

"I am ... I think ... it's like pieces of a large and compli-cated jigsaw puzzle, although I can see now why I couldn't leave and not 'didn't leave'. That is what I have blamed myself for over so many years. I'm hoping in time other pieces will fall into place too." Glancing at the clock Nick said reassuringly,

"All the pieces will fall into place. You are doing really well Kitty, same time next week?"

"Yes thank you." She said. She left the Centre at the top of Morningside Road, feeling she had much to think about.

For the first time Kitty felt the millstone of self-blame lift from her shoulders and from her mind. Somehow she felt lighter and freer than when she had entered the building an hour earlier.

For almost ten years Kitty had blamed herself for not leaving Peter, as if it had been as simple as putting on her coat and saying, "Goodbye Peter, I'm off." She now fully understood that she had been systematically kept in social and geographical isolation, she had been kept without money, she had been stripped of her self confidence and the sense of feeling she was a worthwhile person, as someone who counted. Add fear verging on terror and it wasn't hard to see how much she had been a prisoner in the many homes she had been moved to over the course of a decade. Fear was the tool he had used to ensure her hostage status: fear of violence; fear of what people would say if she told the true circumstances of her life with Peter and fear of censure by a society who finds it more palatable to blame the victims of domestic violence, rather than the perpetrators or the patriarchal society that allows it to exist and continue.

She was glad that she had arranged to meet Kieren for coffee at a lovely old fashioned Tearoom in Bruntsfield Place, the walk there would give her time to reflect on this change of feeling. She and Kieren were becoming close friends, but not too close she thought, not for a while yet.

13

"THEN LIGHT BEGAN TO DAWN AGAIN"

During the thirty minute walk Kitty reflected on her relationship with Kieren and how it began around a year ago. Having moved house yet again, this time back to Edinburgh, Kitty had felt it was time to get out to work and have contact with other people. It had been relatively easy to get Peter to agree as they were desperately short of money with his benefits having been reduced in January of that year.

She set up a private practice in massage and aromatherapy, which she had trained in at the New Zealand College of Massage, and which Peter's manipulation and undermining of her appointments had made it difficult to practice with any regularity. She knew she hadn't lost her skills though, since Peter frequently demanded that she give him a massage. She was extremely fortunate to hire a room within an NHS medical practice in the South Side of Edinburgh. She was very careful to be vague when Peter asked about her work as she didn't want him turning up and causing her trouble, he knew only that she had a room 'somewhere near' Tollcross and that was stretching it a bit. She knew that being in a medical setting was more secure, especially as massage therapists could unwittingly attract the wrong kind of clients. The practice charged her for the room and allowed her to put up a poster advertising her massage and aromatherapy sessions. She offered discount to staff members and some GP's 'referred' patients who were in need of a calming aromatic massage. She loved the social contact with the staff there, it had been such a long time since she'd had any company other than Peter and it was like breathing cool, fresh air after being shut in a putrid environment.

It was there that she had met Kieren Reece on a day when she had been having an unusually late lunch due to a meeting running over. He was a Community Psychiatric Nurse, or CPN for short, and often saw patients within the practice. Kitty had met Kieren on a few previous occasions, always in the company of other members of staff; she knew that he was a popular visitor there and GP's would seek him out for advice on their patients. He was about five, nine tall with a very pleasant appearance and looked fit and healthy, as though he worked out at the gym. His hair was turning from grey to white, a bit like her own, with kind eyes behind the frameless glasses and he had a soothing voice which she imagined would put distressed patients at ease. His eyes were brown and she noticed his long lashes which would be the envy of many women. After chatting about the lovely spring weather, Kitty heard herself ask,

"Would you mind if I asked you a professional question?"

"What would you like to know?" He asked, curious at this turn in the conversation.

"I wanted to ask you about personality disorders." She said and then told him about her life with Peter and that she had been beginning to wonder recently whether such a condition would apply to him. He had long played the 'depression card' and she had put a lot of his behaviour down to that. It was only a couple of days ago, when she had seen her GP, who knew about the abuse, that she began to question the whole thing. The doctor had said categorically, "It's not depression that's causing this behaviour towards you, it's his personality."

For some time afterwards she could hardly believe she had told another person, who was almost a total stranger, what had been going on for a decade. However on closer consideration, she mused it was probably easier to tell someone who was not family or involved in any way. As a taxi driver, she had often found that passengers would impart the most intimate details and worries, knowing that they would in all likelihood, never meet again. That was not an end of it for Kitty though.

When she arrived at work the next day the receptionist handed her a message. It was from Kieren and he had asked her to phone him at his office. Nervously, she made the call. When she was put through to him she said,

"Hello Kieren, I got a message to call you." There was a question in her voice as though she doubted it had been for her. He thanked her for returning his call and said,

"I've been thinking about what you told me yesterday and I thought that you could do with someone to talk to." She was so taken aback that she didn't say anything, so he continued,

"I would be happy to meet with you to talk if you think that would be helpful." She replied,

"Actually, I think it's good idea. Can I think about it and get back to you?" She hadn't at that point wanted to commit to more than that, she needed to think about this and what it meant.

KITTY PUT off contacting Kieren for more than a week, during which time she kept asking herself why was he offering to help her? Did he feel sorry for her? What was his interest in her and, oh my God, did he perhaps fancy her? Her thoughts went in circles for days and then she decided to take his offer at face value. After years of keeping her life a secret it might be therapeutic to get it out into the open, to talk about it to this kind and sympathetic man.

She had arranged to meet him at Crombies Tearoom a week later, the same place she was on her way to now. She remembered how nervous she had been that day, so nervous that her hand shook when she tried to lift the cup of tea to her lips. It took several attempts and then she'd used both hands to steady the cup. She had the strange notion from their previous conversation that he would expect her to have either left Peter or gone to the police. Kieren's next words reassured her that he had no such expectations. This actually confused her; not being judged; not being blamed for having done something 'stupid' or for not having done something. Instead, he had told her about his own situation and how hurt he had been when his wife had said she didn't want him anymore and had told him she wanted him to leave the family home, the home he was paying for, and the children he loved. He had tried so hard to be a good husband and father, but he felt he must have failed if she was telling him to go. This lovely, sensitive man had also been very badly hurt. She wondered if, perhaps, one confidence invited another? Whatever, the outcome was that she no longer felt an object of pity and had enjoyed the rest of their time there.

Not long after the meeting in the tearoom, Kieren invited Kitty to have a meal at his flat and, once again, she wondered was this just as friends and colleagues or was it a date? It transpired that this meal was the night before her fiftieth birthday, the age at which she had promised herself that her life would change. When she arrived at his flat she realised with a pleasure she had not anticipated, that it was a date complete with roses and red wine. Kieren hadn't known about her upcoming birthday and when she told him at midnight he kissed her cheek and wished her a happy birthday.

HER DISCLOSURE at work that day, their conversation at the tearooms and the intimate meal together proved to be a crucial turning point in Kitty's life.

Kitty and Kieren started seeing each other regularly and Kitty found to her great surprise and relief that there were loving and trustworthy men in the world. Her trust in Kieren grew and although she knew she wanted him in her life always, she needed to take it slowly, at least for the time being.

14

"WHEN NORMAL ISN'T NORMAL"

A t her next session Kitty was telling Nick about her reflections on their last meeting. She said,

"I've been thinking about our last session and how we talked about me being trapped in that situation by Peter " Kitty began, "it's so easy to blame myself for what happened and, if I'm not vigilant, it creeps up on me." Nick replied,

"Kitty you have to put the blame squarely where it lies - at Peter's door." She said thoughtfully

"I think it's very much a societal value where the victim of domestic abuse is blamed for 'putting up with it'. I've heard women saying 'I'd be out that door if he laid a finger on me' but it's not that simple, is it? Only women who have never been in an abusive relationship would say that. They can't know how it silently closes in on you and isn't always, or only, physical. This belief in society that women 'get what they deserve by not leaving' is either not acknowledging, or is ignorant of, the patriarchal values endemic in our society and the gender inequalities that underpins them, even now, in the twenty-first century." Nick smiled empathically and said,

"You have certainly been reflecting on a lot since we last met. You're working hard Kitty, not only here but between sessions too." She felt rather pleased by his affirmation of her efforts.

"It's strange now to look back and see how far my life plummeted to a state that became 'normal' in a relatively short time." Nick asked,

"Can you say a bit more about that Kitty?" She replied,

"The violence never became normal; the cracked ribs; the broken finger; the choking and the constant bruises could never become normal, they were something to be feared. No it was the other stuff, the daft schemes to make money rather than get a real job, and somehow, I got sucked into them." She half laughed, half cried, "I became a partner in his 'daftness', it seems so mad now but at the time it was normal, it seemed to make sense." She shook her head at the memory. Nick then asked,

"Have you heard of the Stockholm Syndrome Kitty?" Looking puzzled she replied,

"No, what is it?" Nick told her about it.

"It's a condition where a hostage begins to feel empathy with their captor and is a psychological survival strategy used during captivity." Kitty thought about this for a while and said,

"Yes, it's me being on his side against the world or his parents or anybody he perceived to slight him. Actually, I can see that me agreeing to his schemes, however daft, was my way of trying to survive. Thank you for explaining that Nick, I thought I had become as mad as him. Although I think it may have gone further than that, almost to the point of being 'brainwashed' where I believed it too. I learned quickly not to challenge or question, like the time he believed he could make it to the Commonwealth Games. The truth is, he was never consistent enough in anything to get anywhere." After reflecting a moment Nick said,

"Whether conscious or not, you used these tactics to keep yourself safe and alive." Kitty nodded and said,

"His behaviour got more bizarre as time went on and I often felt embarrassed by him." Nick asked her,

"What do you mean by bizarre?" Kitty heaved a big sigh, considered for a minute then continued,

"It's difficult to know where to start because it sounds like fiction. A lot of it happened during the time that I was part of a team looking after an old lady with dementia. She had a title, I don't recall what it was now, and she lived in a very large house in acres of land."

Kitty went on to tell Nick about how Peter began to tag along when she went to give Mrs A her meals. Tommy, who organised the shifts and had his fingers in many dubious pies, knew him and he wasn't bothered by him hanging around. She recalled,

"Peter got into the habit of wandering about the grounds and outbuildings of the estate while I took Mrs A on outings to the shops and bank. There were also times when Mrs A was away and I would feed the cat and check the house was safe. During those visits Peter scoured the house from top to bottom. The house which had once been very grand with separate staff staircase and accommodation on the top floor, was in a sorry state of disrepair but the risk of rotten floors was no deterrent to him. Peter prowled about the house and went through Mrs A's possessions as he came upon them. In a separate wing of the house he found what must have been Mrs A's husband's bedroom and some personal belongings of his that had been left behind after his death. Eventually

Mrs A went into long term care and my duties were to feed the cat and check the recently installed CCTV. Peter took to going to the house by himself whether I was on duty or not and that's when his behaviour there began to worry me." She sat with the memories for a moment then said,

"He started to bring things home from Mrs A's place." Nick interrupted her,

"You mean he stole things from the old lady's house?" Kitty replied,

"Yes, if you call bringing stacks of *The Times* newspapers dating back to the 1960's stealing."

"What on earth for?" Nick asked. She laughed and said,

"Kindling for life ... no, they would be no good for lighting a fire as most of them were damp and I honestly don't know why he wanted them. It got more serious than bringing rubbish home though, he systematically emptied the large kerosene tank of its contents by siphoning it off into fuel cans and storing them in a cupboard under the stairs." She shuddered at the thought of the fire risk. She held her hand up at Nick's incredulous expression and said, "Before you ask, again I don't know why - we didn't have oil-fired heating. He steadily got worse and one day presented me with a set of beautiful, antique crystal brandy glasses. I told him to take them back, I didn't want what wasn't mine. I can't describe the feeling of total disgust I felt towards him at that moment, but he did take them away, with a bad grace. I don't know whether he returned them to the house or sold them. As if that wasn't bad enough, I arrived one day to find him in Mrs A's safe going through her jewellery. Now that really freaked me out and I begged him to come away." Nick commented on this as gross intrusion. Kitty said,

"He made me feel like an accessory to a crime, his already weak boundaries were disappearing altogether. I gave the job up that day, I felt he was becoming a very loose cannon. I never set foot in the house again." Nick asked,

"Wasn't it risky refusing the crystal and asking him to leave the safe?" Kitty nodded,

"I suppose it was but I had to take the chance. I didn't want to end up in court implicated in theft because of him."

"Perhaps he knew how wrong it was and that's why he didn't react as he might have." Nick observed.

"I don't know Nick ... maybe ... he was always so principled, not to mention hypocritical, when it came to other people's 'wrong doing'. Some time later I found a chair I'd never seen before in the garage of the lodge, it was obviously a souvenir of the Queen's coronation and had a label with Mrs A's husband's name on it. Later still, I discovered it had been smashed to pieces, in what must have been a violent rage. What I do know is, it spurred my desire to leave him. I was becoming aware of how mad this existence was, despite its having been the norm for so long. The continual roller-coaster of actual violence or threats of it, on top of his weird behaviour out in the world, were beginning to grind me down and I would fantasise about him dying and how that 'happy event' would release me from all my problems. There were times when I hated him and my miserable life so much that I became increasingly afraid that I might tip over the edge and stab him in his sleep. I was terrified of ending up in prison like so many women who are driven to killing their tormentors." Nick nodded understanding and said,

"You chose the safer option before the other overtook you." Kitty said,

"Thankfully yes, and I knew I had to get back to Edinburgh to be able to access the support to get away from him and possibly a bolt hole, if necessary." Nick checked the clock before saying,

"We have a few minutes left Kitty, tell me how you managed that."

"Actually, it was easier than I had anticipated, we were struggling financially and I let him think it was his idea to move back to the city where there would be more job opportunities for us both." Nick smiled and said,

"Wise woman! Same time next week?" Kitty agreed, said goodbye and left the centre.

15

ONE YEAR EARLIER

(2004)

Kitty and Peter moved back to Edinburgh in the early spring of 2004. They would have moved before then but finding a flat they could afford had proved harder than expected. Eventually they found a one bedroom flat in a run down part of the city. The flat was furnished, after a fashion, the living room had an aged velour sofa and matching chair which, in better days, would have been described as 'dusky pink'. The curtains and carpet must have been fawn in colour at one time, but were now dirty and faded with years of wear. The only heating in the flat came from a mounted three-bar electric fire on the wall opposite the sofa. The tiny kitchen was in a dingy recess off the living room and a varnished pine table and bench set divided the two living spaces. Looking around her worn shabby surroundings Kitty thought that they were a reflection of herself. She was by then pretty ground down from the difficulties of being married to Peter and looked older than her forty nine years, with almost totally white hair and wearing clothes that were clean, but clearly hand-me-downs. The lines around her eyes had gone from fine laughter lines to those of constant worry. Her small five feet three frame was slightly bowed over from years of physical and emotional ill-use. Peter on the other hand, a well-built man of six feet, in his mid forties with dark hair and skin badly scarred by acne, was a picture of health. His clothes were new and of the casual sweatshirt and joggers type.

Peter found himself a job quickly as the taxi owner he'd worked for previously was looking for a driver. Kitty wondered briefly why he was taking him on again with his unreliable record, then she remembered the owner got his rental fee whether Peter worked or not. She pushed the worry over future debts to the back of her mind and concentrated on her own new business. Kitty had set herself up in Therapeutic Massage and Aromatherapy in the South Side Medical Practice which was situated on Melville Terrace, bordering the Meadows. She loved this area and knew it well from her under and postgraduate years at Edinburgh University. She soon made friends with the practice staff and was able to meet her sisters occasionally during her lunch break without Peter knowing she was having social contact with others. Before long she was making a steady income which would increase as her clientele grew by word of mouth recommendation. She was determined not to let her hard-earned cash be squandered on the debts that had accrued due to Peter's fecklessness. She opened a separate bank account to pay her earnings into. When Peter heard about this he was very angry.

"What do you want to do that for, we've always had a joint account?" He said, feeling threatened by this move towards financial independence. Kitty replied,

"Be reasonable Peter, you know it's overdrawn. I'll pay half of the overdraft and you pay half, then I want my name removed from the account." She thought she was being more than fair since the debts were due to his irregular working pattern. He clearly wasn't happy but didn't argue with her.

For the first few weeks Peter worked regular shifts then reverted to his old ways of taking time off work again. It worried Kitty that he might not be able to pay his share of the rent and bills, but she felt it was pointless to risk an argument as it wouldn't change anything and she could possibly get badly hurt. On the days that Peter stayed home Kitty went off to work not knowing, and past caring about, what he got up to during her absence. There had been a time when his insatiable appetite for pornography had really upset her, but she felt such apathy towards him these days that she didn't have the energy to be curious about what he did, as long as it wasn't under her nose or costing her money.

However, it wasn't long before she found out. The telephone bill arrived one morning and she was surprised to find Peter had already opened it since the account was in her name and was addressed to her. Immediately suspicious, she scrutinised it and saw that two pages of itemised calls were missing. When she mentioned it to him he denied any knowledge of them, saying that's what was in the envelope. She said as casually as she could,

"It must be an administrative error, I'll phone them and get them to send out another as this bill is a lot higher than I was expecting." Whilst he was in the bathroom she searched the bin and found the two missing pages crumpled into a ball. She retrieved them and said nothing to him.

Later at work, during her morning break, she asked some of her colleagues about the call numbers with the extortionate charges. They looked at the bill then exchanged knowing glances, feeling sorry for her naivety, then told her they were 'premium rate' calls, probably to sex lines. Mary, the boldest of her new friends, was already dialling one of the numbers and listened as it was answered. She hung up immediately and confirmed everyone's suspicions. Kitty was not only embarrassed but livid at the deception, not to mention the £300 plus bill which she certainly would not be paying.

WHEN KITTY GOT home that evening she confronted Peter about the bill and told him she knew exactly what those calls were and that she would not be paying a penny of it. It was risky expressing her anger, but she was heart sick of his lies and had known for years that he couldn't be trusted. Caught red-handed he became instantly angry and spat at her accusingly,

"You can't blame me, it's your fault for being so fucking frigid! I can't even touch you but you shout 'inappropriate'. You're my wife and I have rights!" She came back at him with,

"Peter, for heaven's sake, we haven't lived as a married couple for years, we're married on paper only. Your perverse tastes disgust me and it was only ever about you - your wants, your needs, your lusts - I was never considered other than as a vessel for your perversions." Her anger was increasing and she wasn't pulling any punches. She said,

"You have the nerve to call me frigid, well I was never frigid before I met *you*." The disdain dripping from her words was not lost on him. Too late, she realised she should not have engaged in such a heated exchange and knew she had gone too far to retreat, but by now she was so angry.

This lately found confidence of Kitty's enraged Peter and he grabbed her roughly, pulling her down, she felt her ankle crack against the table as she landed awkwardly on the floor. His hands, already around her throat, were squeezing ever more tightly. He snarled,

"Die you bitch, but not before I fuck you!" She struggled ineffectively and then felt herself floating up towards the ceiling of the shabby living room. Looking down on herself being throttled by Peter, she was dreamily aware of talking to her long-dead mother before hitting the floor with a bump, as consciousness returned. She mentally checked out her body, all her clothing was intact, there was no pain other than her ankle and throat. She sighed inwardly with relief that he hadn't raped her as he had threatened. Incapable, she thought, with grim satisfaction.

When she had recovered sufficiently to talk she said to him,

"Do you know I was unconscious, you might have killed me?" His dismissive reply was,

"Don't talk rubbish, your eyes were open all the time." She tried to reason with him,

"Peter, my eyes may have been open but I wasn't conscious, I wasn't here." She waved her arm around the room in emphasis, "You need to get help for these angry episodes."

"It's not me that needs help, it's you! You and your big mouth, you make me angry." He retorted. She left it at that knowing finally that she had to get away from him for good and as soon as possible.

Kitty saw her GP the next day and she told him about the assault. He told her plainly, knowing Peter as a patient of his, that it wasn't depression that was causing his violent behaviour towards her, it was how he was, his personality. Dr Sharp advised her to go to the police, but the mere suggestion filled her with terror. She remembered the many threats of 'you can run but you can't hide' and she knew the police couldn't protect her twenty four hours a day. No, she had to get away and not let him know where.

IT WAS LATER that week that she had the fortuitous conversation with Kieren about Peter's possible personality disorder and his phone call to her the next day, offering to meet up and talk about her situation. After the conversation in the tearooms they had met socially on a couple of occasions. It wasn't long after she and Kieren began dating that she felt a shift in the power relationship between herself and Peter. She was aware that she no longer felt afraid of him and had even told him she was seeing someone. There was something about the way he accepted this news that she felt safely out of his reach and out of the sphere of his power and influence. She also informed him that she was leaving and applying for divorce and expected him to sign and return the divorce papers without delay. By this time she had found a room in a house in a good part of Edinburgh where she thought she'd feel safe enough to start getting her life back together again. She arranged to move when he was at work, at least she hoped he would go to work, that day of all days. Fortunately he did go to work and Kieren arrived to help her move the few possessions she had.

She had wondered whether Peter's lack of threatening behaviour and apparent cooperation in the run up to her departure, were due to the fact that he perceived her as 'belonging' to another man; someone else's 'property', which is how he would look at it. She really didn't care what he thought, what was important was that she had found the key to her prison and she was now free of Peter Parnell.

16

"BODY MEMORIES: UNWANTED LEGACY"

A t her next session, Kitty told Nick in detail about the move to Edinburgh from the country the previous year, their search for somewhere to live and subsequent violent incident. She continued with her account,

"I was keen to get back to the city where there would be the help and support I would need to finally leave Peter and his 'madness'. My original idea had been to get my business started and take some time to make proper plans for leaving, you know, getting a flat in a nice area and bits and pieces for it, but his violence that day was so frightening that I had to move quickly." Nick nodded and said,

"Kitty, that was a horrendous attack on you and, as you correctly told him, he could have killed you. What men like Peter fail to realise is that it is very easy to kill someone unintentionally by choking them. I have to tell you that your 'talking' to your dead mother sounds to me like a 'near death' experience. If he'd squeezed your throat any longer you may well not be sitting here now." Kitty shuddered at the thought and said,

"It did seem strange at the time that I was talking to my mother, but I never thought about it in that way. I just thought it was a 'floaty' part of being unconscious." Nick continued,

"If he hadn't loosened his grip when he did, he could be serving a prison sentence."

"Speaking to my GP and Kieren afterwards accelerated my plan of action. Apart from the trauma itself, it was as though I'd had an epiphany." Kitty said shaking her head, "everything came into sharp focus - the years of misery because of his so called mental illness were nothing other than the depraved actions of a man with a pathological personality." Nick agreed,

"It can happen like that when, suddenly you see the situation clearly and what you need to do. I don't believe a complete break from him would have been possible in the country where you were so socially and geographically isolated. You alluded to that yourself when you took the opportunity of his absence that Christmas to gather information about services that could help you when the time came." Kitty went on,

"The support of my colleagues when I disclosed the abuse was immediate and genuinely reassuring. The friendship of Kieren was paramount in me regaining some of my lost self confidence and self esteem in the months that followed, although I'm still struggling with certain things a year on. For example, I can't wear polo neck jumpers or clothes and jewellery high up around my throat without feeling like I'm being choked. If my coat is buttoned right up and I'm walking, that's okay, but the minute I sit down and it presses against my throat I panic and have to undo the buttons immediately to free my neck of constriction. It's the feeling of panic that bothers me, it's not a rational thought process where I register the tightness and then loosen it. There's a desperation to be free, as though I might die otherwise." Nick said,

"What you're experiencing Kitty is called a 'body memory'. This often happens when a person has experienced serious trauma to a particular part of their body. Sometimes, even years later, after working through the emotional and psychological effects of the trauma the body still remembers it. The memory has been retained at a cellular level in that part of the body, so it's no wonder that you panic and fear you may die. I'm sorry to say that, in all probability, it will not go away. However, you can reduce, or even free yourself from the panic by being mindful and taking steps to consciously prevent it happening." Kitty looked downcast and said,

"So I'm stuck with it?" Nick replied,

"You're already learning to live with it by choosing clothes and jewellery that won't trigger the memory or by fastening them in a way that doesn't constrict your throat. I know it doesn't seem fair, but look at it from the bigger picture - you're still alive and you got away." Kitty agreed,

"You're absolutely right Nick and it was one of his favourite methods of shutting me up. There was one occasion when I didn't try to resist. I was in the shower after he had thrown a plate of food all over me and I just didn't have the energy or desire to resist. I went limp and he very quickly stopped squeezing my throat, I think he thought he'd killed me. The next day I could hardly swallow because of the agonising pain and it felt as though something had broken, although what could break there I don't know." Nick cut in saying,

"Actually the muscles there protect the trachea from damage when being choked and letting them go limp is probably what caused the pain. The power to control a person's next breath makes strangulation or choking a common tactic for abusers. Consciousness is lost in less than 10 seconds and death can occur in under five minutes. Most abusers don't strangle or choke to kill but to show their partners that they *can* kill." Kitty sighed,

"So I did the wrong thing, I never tried it again as the pain was so frightening." Nick said,

"Don't be so hard on yourself Kitty, it sounds as though it was effective in getting him to stop." She said,

"It was also effective in sabotaging a meeting I was to go to the next evening. I was to give a talk to a group my sister Anna went to and, obviously, I had to cancel as I was in so much pain. He sabotaged a lot of my plans, now I think about it. He once put my folding massage table, that I had made specially for me in New Zealand, on top of the wardrobe when he knew a client was coming. I had to cancel as there was no way I could get it down safely by myself. I made some lame excuse, I could hardly tell her the truth, could I? What a bastard, what an unconscionable bastard!" she said angrily. Nick nodded approvingly,

"That's good Kitty, you need to be in touch with your anger towards him. The once paralysing fear you felt has given way to righteous anger. I believe the anger was there all the time, but fear was the overriding emotion." Kitty said,

"Anytime I had the nerve or was unwise enough to vent anger was met by more violence. He always made me 'pay for it'."

"Knowing that 'survival is the best revenge', Kitty told Nick about the meeting with Kieren the previous year and their subsequent on-going relationship over that time and how this had been a huge part of her recovery before therapy. "He has helped me to exorcise my demons by his kindness, patience and very gentle nature. I still have some way to go and it took me months to stop apologising to people. I would say sorry to Kieren if I thought I'd shut the car door too hard, or if I didn't shut it properly. It was the same with other people in different situations. I know now it was because of years of walking on eggshells with Peter. Thankfully it doesn't happen now unless there is something to apologise for. He is the opposite of everything Peter was … and probably still is." She told Nick in wonder, almost unable to believe her good fortune to have met such a man. "There isn't a day goes by but I pinch myself to make sure he's real and I'm not just dreaming." Nick smiled and said,

"I'm so pleased for you Kitty, you deserve to be happy after the hell you've been through with Peter."

"Thanks Nick" she said, "I'm starting to think of that period as the 'Dark Decade' which is well and truly over, despite the recurring nightmares." Nick stated simply,

"They will go over time Kitty as you continue to regain your emotional and psychological strength and as your trust in Kieren deepens. You know he is a good man." Smiling, Kitty replied,

"I do indeed." Looking at the clock on the table Nick said,

"I think you have made excellent progress in the time you have been coming here Kitty and we are, perhaps, coming to the end of your need for therapy. I would usually continue working over a longer period with a woman who has suffered this kind of trauma. However, I believe that the positive regard and respect that some women need to gain from continuing therapy is something you get daily from Kieren. Your relationship with him is very strong, healing, and extremely affirming for you, especially so after your existence with Peter. Think about what I've said over the coming week and, if you are agreeable, we will work towards ending your therapy over two or three more sessions." Kitty exhaled a long breath and asked,

"Will that he discharge or 'graduation'?" Smiling, Nick replied,

"Oh it's definitely graduation! Kitty, you have been remarkable in your commitment to the therapy process, it's hard work and you have put so much energy and effort into it. Same time next week?" Smiling from ear to ear she said,

"Absolutely!"

17

"SURVIVAL IS THE BEST REVENGE"

K itty was beginning to relax properly and was, for the first time in over a decade, thoroughly enjoying life. It was wonderful to feel safe again, despite the recurring nightmare which was happening less frequently and with fewer lasting effects on waking. She felt the trauma of her life with Peter was beginning to recede and she no longer feared an unexpected visit from him. She was no longer in his thrall, no longer afraid. Fear, she was beginning to realise, had been her prison bars, a prison of his making. She thought back to the times when he had held the door wide open, taunting her to go, and she now knew clearly why she could not step over the threshold. Well no more!

She was seeing Kieren twice a week now, on Tuesdays and Fridays, which fitted in with his time for seeing his children and for going to the gym after work. He liked to exercise and was, indeed, fitter than many men half his age. They were so comfortable with each other now and she smiled when she remembered her first meal with Kieren. He had asked her to tell him about herself and she couldn't think of anything to say, her mind had gone totally blank. She felt she had nothing interesting to say, nobody had shown an interest in her for such a long time. Suddenly, she had a flash of inspiration, something had triggered her mind back to her world trip. She became enthusiastic, animated was how Kieren had described her later. That little 'pilot light' of her former self had ignited into full flame. This was a real turning point, a return of the 'Kitty who had donned a backpack and travelled the world on her own', as her friend Charles had said to her on one of his clandestine visits. Peter had hated Charles with a passion because he was gay, but he would visit when Kitty phoned to say Peter had definitely gone out to work. Of course, it was much easier these days since meeting Charles didn't have to be a secret. Kieren had met Charles on several occasions and they had got on well with each other.

As Kitty had only a room in a house, she and Kieren would often spend their evenings together at Kieren's flat where he would cook delicious meals for them. She loved the space he had created for himself, with one wall lined with books, whilst his music collection, comprising of CD's, tapes and vinyl was eclectic. He had introduced Kitty to a range of genres that greatly widened her experience of music. She realised that with Peter, there was no music and no soul.

With mutual, tacit agreement, Kitty and Kieren were taking their relationship at a slow pace. Neither of them wanted to rush into it because of their past experiences. Kieren had been badly hurt, feeling rejected after years of lovingly and conscientiously looking after and providing for his wife and children. It transpired that he was 'surplus to requirement' once the long asked for and long coveted house had been bought. It was understandable that he was wary of falling into a similar situation again. Kitty, aware of this and who couldn't be more different from his ex-wife, didn't lay any such demands on him.

As time went by, the ice which Kieren said had enveloped his heart to protect him from further hurt, gradually melted and allowed him to fully embrace the love that Kitty offered him. She had known instinctively (her instincts were returning) that he needed time to heal from the devastating betrayal and rejection by his wife. Kitty knew from their conversations that work had been his salvation, he had concentrated his energies on people who needed him. It had given him a sense of continuing purpose in life, which he had lost as a husband and father; a reason to get up in the morning. His contact with his children, a son and a daughter, had been greatly reduced, seeing them much more infrequently than when living in the family home. Again tacitly, Kitty respected his need to keep her and his children separate for the time being, understanding that he did not want to introduce her as a new person in his life until he was sure their relationship would be enduring and permanent.

THEY WERE both surprised at how they came to be together at that particular point in their lives, a time when it had been crucial for Kitty. She believed that Kieren had rescued her, 'her knight on a white charger', although his 'charger' had actually been a red Mini One. As time went by and they grew closer to each other, Kitty discovered that Kieren felt she had rescued him by helping to heal the pain which had been embedded in his heart and allowing him the joy of loving again and of being in love.

At times Kitty would look back and marvel at how, with

all the twists and turns in their separate lives, they had come together in the staff room of the South Side Medical Practice at the exact same time. When in fanciful mood, she would look on it as Fate putting them on a meticulously planned course to be in the same place at the same time when nobody else would be there and she shuddered slightly at the thought of the Dark Decade being part of her 'destiny'. She wasn't at all sure if she liked this idea; what if she'd done something different at one point, would that have changed everything? She couldn't bear the thought that she might never have met Kieren. Then her logical mind would take over, acknowledging that Fate knew what she was doing when plotting people's destinies, paying attention to each and every turn on the road from birth to this very moment, hence the Dark Decade being a part of it.

Although her life with Peter was total deprivation of many things ... individual freedom, self confidence, self worth, financial independence ... now she was out of it, safely on the other side, she wondered whether she could use her own personal experience to help others. How did the self help books put it? Turning a bad experience into something positive, or words to that effect. The psychological, and sometimes literally the physical, smothering at Peter's hands had given her a profound understanding of how and why women in abusive relationships could not 'just leave him', could not just walk out of the door. The fear generated by this kind of trauma bypasses the 'fight or flight' said to be the two possible responses to danger and moves to a 'freeze' response. She had found scientific references to this newly recognised phenomenon which is a product of an ancient part of the human brain when a person finds themselves in a dangerous or life threatening situation. This new information was greatly comforting to Kitty in that it underlined the fact that it was not weakness that had kept her in that situation. The more information she uncovered the more she understood about the intricacies and levels of abusive and coercive control.

Her sisters had certainly taken to Kieren. Helena had whispered that she thought he was handsome and Kitty knew Anna approved of him because he was in a profession and, as such, had a steady job and any comparison with an unnamed person would remain unspoken. If her sisters were aware of Kitty changing from being strained and always on edge to being relaxed and carefree, they never verbalised it, they just saw Kitty as being back to her old self. She hadn't told them about the true nature of her life with Peter, but she would one day, when she felt the time was right.

18

"LIKE A BAD PENNY"

Kitty walked down the steps of the South Side Medical Practice after work one early autumn evening. The sinking sun, still warm, cast a golden glow on the ancient trees that lined the Meadows and Melville Drive. She took a contented breath of air and then stopped suddenly in her tracks. Standing on the pavement watching her was Peter, now her ex since the divorce came through a year before. She asked calmly but curtly,

"What are you doing here and how did you know where I'd be?" He tapped the side of his nose, in ridiculous theatrical manner, and said,

"Ah, you have to be a detective to find the elusive Kitty Dawson." Smugness spreading across his unpleasant face. Kitty replied,

"I hardly think so, it's more likely that you happened to see me while you were driving the taxi and followed me." As an afterthought she added, "That by the way, is stalking, hence illegal." The smugness gave way to another emotion and she wondered what it was - worry, fear? It was obviously something unpleasant from the way his face changed so quickly.

"I need your help." Kitty started walking away quickly, saying over her shoulder,

"No! Go away! I finished with you a long time ago, you're on your own." Moving deftly Peter stood in front of her, blocking her way. She wasn't afraid, merely exasperated. Before she could say anything else he said,

"I'm in trouble with the police." Kitty retorted,

"Oh, so your crimes have caught up with you at last! Which poor sod did you beat up this time for trying to 'bump' you for the fare?" Startled by this response he took a half step backwards, he'd forgotten the time he'd come home from a night shift with bloody and bruised knuckles from 'punishing' a drunk who'd tried giving him the slip, rather than hand over the amount on the meter. He said,

"The police said they'd be talking to you soon to give them a statement. I'm due in court next month. My defence lawyer will also be contacting you at this address." He nodded his head in the direction of the medical practice she had just left.

Kitty stopped trying to get away and demanded an explanation of why he was involving her in this since she hadn't seen him in the last year and a half. Bloody hell, she thought, just when my life is going fine and he's well and truly out of it, this! He looked at her desperately and said,

"It's about Mrs A's stuff, you remember Jenny? Well she sold the house and when she was clearing it out she noticed that some of Mrs A's things were missing and they're pointing the finger at me, you've got to help me." Kitty said,

"So what concern is that of mine? I told you to take the stuff back. Those crystal brandy glasses were probably heirlooms, no wonder Jenny missed them and no, I don't have to help you!" He rushed on,

"I need you to say that I never had anything of hers, please!" The 'please' faintly amused her as it had never been part of his vocabulary before.

"You knew exactly what you were doing, you just couldn't keep your hands off her property, thought it was fair game to steal from a demented old woman, a demented, rich old woman. You must have sold or used the kerosene by now - and the crystal glasses? Sold to Christie's or pawned for what you could get for them? What about the Coronation chair you smashed to firewood, is Jenny missing that too?" She snorted in disgust.

The pavement was busy with people going home from work or lectures at the university nearby, and who looked curiously at the two people, obviously arguing but oblivious to them, as they tried to make their way around them. He shook his head and said,

"It's the missing jewellery." Holding her hand up in a motion for him to stop talking she said angrily.

"Don't tell me any more! I don't want to know. I'm not lying for you, I'm not committing perjury to save your lying, thieving arse!" She walked off in the opposite direction of home, towards her sister Denise's flat at Tollcross, so she could regain her equilibrium. She didn't look back until she had gone some way and was relieved he wasn't following her.

WHEN KITTY ARRIVED at work one morning a week later, she was given an envelope that had been left for her at reception. She waited until she was in her therapy room before opening it. As she had guessed, it was from the police requesting her presence at the local police station to give them a statement regarding the case against Peter Parnell which would be going to court soon. Kitty decided to go after work that evening and get it over with, although she wasn't looking forward to it or having to recall her life with Peter. It was one thing talking to Nick, but this made her feel somehow tainted by association.

Kitty walked into St Leonard's police station around 5.30pm and handed the notice requesting her presence to the desk sergeant. After a few minutes wait a young female police officer showed her into an interview room which was windowless, painted grey and empty apart from the screwed down table and chairs. They sat on either side of the table and the officer, who introduced herself as Gillian Evans, informed Kitty about the charges against her ex-husband. These included: the theft of a diamond and sapphire pendant valued at £10,000, along with rings, brooches and other items of jewellery to the value of £150,000. Some of the items had been found in an upmarket pawnbroker on the corner of Queen Street and North Castle Street in the city's West End. The owner of the premises was able to describe the person who 'pledged' the items and had said that he didn't see jewellery of that quality every day. Although he was a bit suspicious at first, he had taken them from the man who said they'd been left to him by a late aunt. He was able to identify Peter from the police photos and had agreed to testify in court. Mrs A's niece had provided photos of the missing jewellery, which had been taken years before for insurance purposes, and the pawn-broker confirmed that they were the pieces pledged. The officer continued,

"Mr Parnell has stated to investigating officers that you could vouch for him to the effect that he had never removed anything from Forestdean House whilst employed there to check on security. Is that true?" Kitty was very angry at being manipulated and implicated in his nefarious schemes and told the officer about her life with Peter and how he had brought some of Mrs A's possessions home, emphasising the fact that she had told him to return them right away, whether he did she had no way of knowing. She went on,

"By this time Mrs A had been in a care home for some time and we were feeding her cat and checking the security of the house. I was absolutely appalled one day, when I turned up to check the house and CCTV, to find him inside the walk-in safe. He wasn't even supposed to be there that day. I wanted him to get out at once. He said he was 'just looking' and eventually came away closing it behind him. I resigned that evening as I was afraid of being implicated in anything criminal. I don't know how he got into the safe, whether by key or combination lock."

The officer had written down Kitty's statement verbatim and, two and a half hours later, read it back to her and asked her to initial every page. She concluded the interview by saying that the case against Peter was being regarded as particularly serious, as the crimes were against a vulnerable old lady who had trusted him.

When Kitty got home she felt as though she had been through a mangle. She was totally drained after giving her statement to the police. She had been informed that she would receive a citation to attend the court as a witness for the prosecution when the case came to trial. She'd also been told there was a very small chance that Peter might change his plea to 'guilty', in which case she would not be called to give evidence. She was sure he would never admit guilt and would hold out until the bitter end. At that moment she felt extremely angry with Peter Parnell and thought, after going through hell at his hands for years and finally getting away and having her life how she wanted it, feeling safe and happy, he rears his ugly head again, bastard that he is!

The following week Kitty was contacted by Peter's defence solicitor, a George Barclay of Barclay, Barclay and Cohen Solicitors at 20b Grassmarket, Edinburgh. After talking to Kitty for a short time, it became evident that she would not be a reliable witness for the defence as she would be telling the court the truth about her marriage to Peter Parnell and his dubious actions.

KITTY FOUND the following five weeks very difficult with the prospect hanging over her of telling a court full of people about her life with Peter and her suspicions of his criminal activities. Her sleep was disturbed by restless dreams of Peter helping himself to Mrs A's property and herself being interviewed by the police, accused of being an accomplice. She would waken up from these dreams in a cold sweat and curse Peter Parnell to perdition all over again. She knew that if it hadn't been for Kieren's reassuring, steady presence and having the opportunity of talking the whole nasty matter through with Nick, she would have been in a terribly agitated state and unable to function properly. As it was, she was managing to stay calm by telling herself that it would soon be over as they were already into October.

It was the middle of the month when Kitty received the good news. The evidence against Peter was sufficiently damning that his lawyer advised him to change his plea to guilty, thereby hopefully reducing any sentence being handed down. Sheriffs and Judges did not take kindly to the accused wasting court time by insisting on a trial by jury when the evidence against them would clearly lead to a conviction. The Procurator Fiscal was confident that Peter would be given a custodial sentence. Kitty was so relieved and she called Kieren straight away to tell him the wonderful news.

19

"AS YOU SOW, SO SHALL YOU REAP"

I t was Kitty's final therapy session and she was thanking Nick for helping her get her old self and her life back again. Nick said,

"Kitty you may not realise it, but you had already come a long way along the road to recovery when you walked through that door. You were beginning to heal due to these positive changes in your life: you got away from Peter to a place of safety; you're doing the work you love that you had trained for all those years ago and your relationship with Kieren, which I believe has been a crucial factor in you recovering your self confidence, sense of self worth and being able to trust again in an intimate way. You knew you needed help with the niggling, remaining issues such as self-blame, which is so common amongst survivors of domestic abuse. How do you feel about this being your last session?

"In fine with it, now the prospect of giving evidence in court has gone. A few weeks ago I wouldn't have been so confident and thank you for extending the sessions until the crisis was over." She handed Nick a newspaper cutting and said, "I don't know if you've seen this, it's the report of the trial and his sentencing."

THE REPORT, which was published in the Edinburgh Evening News of 20 October 2005, follows:

REPORT OF THE TRIAL IN THE
EDINBURGH EVENING NEWS

"Local Man Convicted Of 'Heinous Crime' Against
Vulnerable Octogenarian

Peter Parnell of 23 Meadow Mews, Preston Village, East Lothian, has been found guilty at Edinburgh Sheriff Court of the theft of jewellery to the value of £150,000. Parnell, 44 and part time Edinburgh taxi driver, was accused under Solemn Procedure, of stealing various items of jewellery, including a rare sapphire and diamond pendant (a family heirloom), from the safe in the home of Mrs X, who cannot be named for legal reasons, whilst employed to check the security of the house and estate after Mrs X had gone into a care home suffering advanced dementia and could no longer be looked after at home.

It was only when Mrs X's home was sold in 2004 that her niece discovered that some of her Aunt's jewellery was missing, along with sundry other items. The high valuation of the missing jewellery had taken police enquiries to Mathieson & Reynolds, an upmarket pawnbroker in the city's New Town. They received confirmation there that Parnell, identified from police photos, had pledged several pieces of expensive jewellery. The pawnbroker, who had been suspicious at first, was convinced by a smartly dressed Parnell that he had inherited them from his late Aunt and was pawning them as he'd fallen on hard times. All of the items were in their original velvet or leather boxes and the police had found that the fingerprints on them and the safe matched those of Parnell.

Initially Parnell denied all charges and made a plea of 'not guilty'. However, the prosecution heard evidence from a reliable witness stating that he, Parnell, had been seen in Mrs X's safe 'going through her jewellery' and had seen, on another occasion, other items of hers in his possession. This witness also remains anonymous for legal reasons. Consequently, Parnell's defence solicitor, Mr George Barclay of Barclay, Barclay and Cohen, advised Parnell to change his plea to guilty, due to the evidence against him and in the hope of receiving a lighter sentence.

At the trial, Sheriff Mrs Margaret-Ann Davidson, in a brief summing up stated: "You have admitted guilt to a despicable, heinous crime against an extremely vulnerable old lady whose trust you have so callously abused. Taking your change of plea to 'guilty' into consideration, thereby potentially saving the Court time and resources, the sentence would normally be less than if found guilty by a jury. However, notwithstanding the guilty plea, you waited until the last minute to change it, hence incurring much time and effort by the police and Procurator Fiscal. Therefore, as an example and deterrent to others who may be inclined to prey on the vulnerable, I am imposing the maximum sentence permitted. Peter Parnell I sentence you to eight years imprisonment with a release date no earlier than 31 May 2013, despite 'good behaviour' indicating an earlier release date." Parnell, paling visibly, was led down to the cells to await being transported to prison."

Nick said,

"Justice seems to have been done for Mrs A, you and hopefully other potential victims. How do you think you'll feel when his release date eventually comes round?" Kitty replied,

"I have thought about that and I'm not worried. He now knows that he can no longer bully me and I'm sure, after his time in prison, he will not be in a hurry to repeat the experience." Nick nodded and said,

"Well done Kitty, you have survived Peter Parnell and you are thriving wonderfully. It's been an honour to work with such a courageous woman." Kitty blushed and said,

"Thank you so much Nick, you have made all the difference. Actually, I have some good news for you ... Kieren and I are engaged" she flashed the diamond ring he hadn't noticed, "and we are going to be married in May next year." She stood up to leave and Nick came across the room and hugged her warmly, saying,

"Congratulations Kitty, I love a happy ending!" Kitty laughed and, having the last word said,

"It's also a happy beginning!"

EPILOGUE

MAY 2006

On Saturday 20th May at 2.30pm, Kitty and Kieren were married in the 15th Century Rosslyn Chapel. In the midst of the exquisitely carved pillars and before friends and family, they pledged their love for and lifelong commitment to each other, through the joys and sorrows that life brings to everyone. Kitty was stunning in a simple ivory silk dress with a beautiful Swarovski Crystal tiara in her hair. Kieren, so handsome in his suit and bow tie, was obviously very moved as he watched his bride walking up the aisle looking radiantly happy. As the happy couple posed for their wedding photos beneath the beautiful May blossom, they both remembered the spring two years earlier, when they first met at the South Side Medical Practice.

THE END

ABOUT THE AUTHOR

Kay Race was born in Edinburgh in 1954 where she grew up. She was educated at Edinburgh University both as an undergraduate and postgraduate. She now lives happily in Northumberland with her husband and two sight hounds, Poppet the whippet and rescue greyhound Bertie.

If you want to know when my next book is due go to www.creaking-chair-books.com and sign up for email updates.

Follow Kay on Twitter@KayRace2

 twitter.com/Twitter@KayRace2

ACKNOWLEDGEMENTS

Firstly I would like to thank Gillian Ashley for the time and commitment she has contributed in editing the manuscript and for making it a better book to read, I could not have gone so far without her assistance.

My thanks also go to authors Gary Dolman and Stuart Wheatman for their patience and support of a novice author.

I wish to thank HHJ R Shetty, for his advice on the justice system and sentencing.

Last, but certainly not least, my thanks to my wonderful husband Keith who very patiently removed himself upstairs to allow me exclusive use of my 'writing room', otherwise known as the living room.

HELPFUL INFORMATION

If you have been affected by domestic abuse, sexual violence or coercive control you can access advice, support and information on the following 24 hour/7 days a week free helplines

Scottish Women's Aid 0800 027 1234

National Women's Aid: 0808 2000 247
    Women's Aid Wales: 0808 80 10 800
    Women's Aid Northern Ireland: 0808 802 141

Note

From 1st October, the Right to Ask Disclosure Scheme will be rolled out to the whole of Scotland (previously trialled in Aberdeen and Ayrshire). Under this scheme women and men have the right to ask about the background of a partner, a potential partner or the partner of someone they know. Go to scotland.police.uk for more information and application form.

A similar scheme is in place in England and Wales called The Domestic Violence Disclosure Scheme (also called Clare's Law) and is operated by police forces there.

Printed in Great Britain
by Amazon